"I'm afraid of getting involved with you."

Lorelei looked down at her shoes, sure she had been transported into someone else's body. Men like Chris Jansen did not say these things to women like her. The woman he should have been saying them to would have known how to reply. But the shoes were hers, and the ineptness was hers, as well. "That's very flattering, but you shouldn't tease me like that, Chris."

His eyes widened in surprise. "Tease you?"

"I'm not fishing for compliments or anything, but I'm hardly the kind of woman who... I mean I've never kept anyone awake nights..."

"Are you so sure? That's another one of our problems—you don't have any idea what you do to me." He took hold of her hands again and slowly pulled her to him. "Hasn't anyone ever thrown your life off center, Lorelei?"

Dear Reader:

The spirit of the Silhouette Romance Homecoming Celebration lives on as each month we bring you six books by continuing stars!

And we have a galaxy of stars planned for 1988. In the coming months, we're publishing romances by many of your favorite authors such as Annette Broadrick, Sondra Stanford and Brittany Young. Beginning in January, Debbie Macomber has written a trilogy designed to cure any midwinter blues. And that's not all—during the summer, Diana Palmer presents her most engaging heros and heroines in a trilogy that will be sure to capture your heart.

Your response to these authors and other authors of Silhouette Romances has served as a touchstone for us, and we're pleased to bring you more books with Silhouette's distinctive medley of charm, wit and—above all—romance.

I hope you enjoy this book and the many stories to come. Come home to romance—for always!

Sincerely,

Tara Hughes
Senior Editor
Silhouette Books

LYNNETTE MORLAND

Mid-Air

Published by Silhouette Books New York

America's Publisher of Contemporary Romance

SILHOUETTE BOOKS
300 E. 42nd St., New York, N.Y. 10017

Copyright © 1987 by Karen O'Connell

ISBN: 0-373-08548-6

First Silhouette Books printing December 1987

America's Publisher of Contemporary Romance

Printed in the U.S.A.

Books by Lynnette Morland

Silhouette Romance

Occupational Hazard #339
Camera Shy #399
Irish Eyes #432
Magic City #443
No Questions Asked #483
Mid-Air #548

LYNNETTE MORLAND

lives in New York and considers it the most glorious city in the universe (although she plans to give London a chance to snatch the title). She loves antique clothing, drinking espresso in Greenwich Village cafés, reading in bed and staying up all night to write her books.

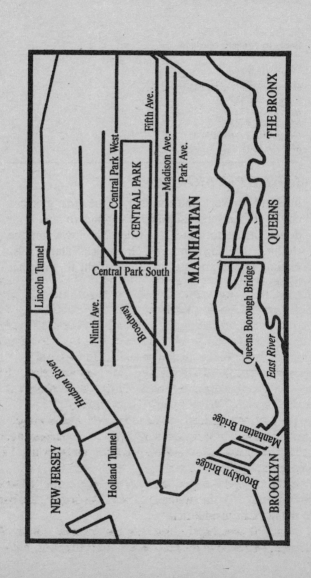

Chapter One

Lorelei looked at her clipboard and ignored the whirling of her head. A major concert was always just one step away from pandemonium, but as an assistant producer she was used to it. She called through the door of the dank cinder-block dressing room and told everyone to pull on their clothes. She gave them a few seconds, then walked in.

"Okay, you guys are on next. Is everyone here?" She counted heads: a drummer, two guitarists, a sax player...but no lead singer. "What'd you do with Mickey?"

The thin young men looked sheepish, and a couple of their equally thin girlfriends giggled. The manager pulled the house telephone away from his face to answer her. "He went back to get his guitar."

In the ninety-six-degree heat, Lorelei felt a chill. "He went back *where*?" To the equipment truck, she prayed, not back to the hotel in Manhattan.

"Back to the hotel. Hey, it's his favorite guitar. We thought we had it in the limo when we came down, but—"

Lorelei held up her hand to silence his explanation. "Exactly *when* did Mickey leave?"

"Oh, could be an hour by now, in the limo. Don't worry, he's never missed a gig—not entirely, anyway."

"I certainly hope not," she said with a bright, strained smile. Be cool, she told herself. Never ruffle the talent. "Look, you all just relax and wait for him. When he shows up, you send a runner to the command center, right? And you contact me on that walkie-talkie. Press the button to talk, take your finger off the button to listen." They all nodded condescendingly, but Lorelei knew they'd never remember her instructions. Electronic geniuses, they could self-produce state-of-the-art digital recordings of music synthesized on a Fairlight computer, but they'd have trouble working a telephone made of two paper cups and a string—she'd have bet her job on it.

Bad choice of words—if she let the concert bog down over one missing act, she'd *lose* her job. Worse things had happened, she reminded herself. At least everyone in this band was still alive. She flipped through the pages on her clipboard looking for the limousine assignments; first she would try to contact Mickey's driver on his car phone....

She backed into what felt like a wall of muscle. As she whipped around, apologizing, hands reached out to steady her. The sight of the man she had rammed caused her "I'm sorry!" to die away. He looked as if he had wandered in from...from...her imagination failed her. From someplace where the major form of exercise was not hoisting a few brews and the principal foods were not cold pizza and warm cola. Vitality and an easy masculine strength radiated from him like heat. His heavy, tawny gold hair waved away from his face unwillingly, as if he had to force it with impatient fingers. His golden skin glowed in the dim corridor like a stray patch of sunlight. Instead of the usual jeans, he wore an oatmeal-colored suit with the jacket tossed over one shoulder and a vivid blue sleeveless T-shirt that lay like silk across his broad, muscular chest. Aside from being well-groomed, he was a good ten to fifteen years older than most of the people backstage, yet he had a bright orange back-stage badge clipped to his belt. It was the ultimate access pass: it would allow him to swing from the rafters above the stage if he chose to. One hundred twenty-seven people—an unmanageably high number due to the size of the all-day concert—were entitled to those orange passes. Lorelei had drawn up the list herself, and she knew every person on it. Yet she didn't know him. She sighed. Someone had been switching badges again or, worse, *selling* them. In her world, backstage passes were more valuable than gold.

However this man had gotten hold of a badge, the twin-kle in his deep-set blue eyes drove out all her thoughts of questioning him. When he grinned, his face turned into a marvelous study of dimples and laugh lines. Lorelei had never before noticed how a few years' worth of seasoning could add so much interest to a man's face.

"I'm looking for Lorelei Chant," he announced in a deep, gravelly voice.

It took her a moment to realize he had said her own name. "Oh! That's me. Sorry."

"Sorry? *I'm* not sorry."

"I mean for bumping you . . . I'm sorry." She was also ri-diculously flustered. She had fought with the biggest rock stars, sweet-talked press potentates, advised the directors of record companies and stadiums, yet this man seemed to have made her wits evaporate. "What can I do for you?" That sounded fairly normal, she decided.

Before he could answer, a horn honked at Lorelei's back. She jumped and saw one of the golf carts used to transport VIPs through the cavernous backstage area. It was driven by a middle-aged man in a jogging suit. His thin reddish-gray hair stuck out like wire.

"Is this concert over for you or something, Lori? I'm not paying you to schmooze, you know." He executed a rough

U-turn in the corridor, jouncing hard over a bundle of cables, scattering a group of roadies and finally speeding back into the bowels of the stadium.

Lorelei sighed. "That was my boss."

The blond man's dark brows compressed his narrow eyes even further. "That's Gil Gilman? The producer of this concert?"

"The very same." She shook herself. Gil had been right, despite his abrasive manner; she had no business standing around basking in the presence of this splendid man while the concert fell apart. "I'm kind of in the middle of a small crisis right now, Mr.— I'm sorry, what is your name?"

"Christian."

As in Fletcher Christian? she wondered, savoring the name. "Ah. Well, do you *desperately* need to talk to me right now, Mr. Christian? Or can you wait until we can sit somewhere in peace?"

"Christian is my *first* name—Chris. And I can wait as long as necessary, but it took me forty-five minutes to find you in this place. Do you mind if I tie a string to you?"

"Or maybe I could leave a trail of bread crumbs? Tell you what, Chris, you can follow me if you want." Then she grinned, feeling an unexpected tickle of flirtatiousness surfacing. "If you can keep up."

He raised an eyebrow. "Oh, I can keep up."

It turned out that he could indeed. In fact, Lorelei found that the mysterious Chris made better sense of the war zone backstage than many a scarred veteran. The hysteria rolled off him like rain off a roof, and the posturing and snobbish attitudes left him unimpressed. He carried with him such an air of imperturbable good humor that people seemed to calm down when he walked into a room. And the effect he had on women! Lorelei had never met a man who, without the aid of bizarre hair or tight leather pants, could turn the head of every female he passed. Chris could and did. Who was this man? she asked herself urgently. Chris who?

Over the next hour she took him from dressing room to office to restricted elevator, all through the echoing passageways that honeycombed Giants Stadium. While the worst congestion occurred down below, near the loading dock and the ramp to the stage, the worst emotional scenes took place in the secluded lounges and VIP rooms farther back.

The concert had been going on for five hours. Seven acts had played; four remained. Everything was happening right on time according to the schedule Lorelei had issued to the performers. According to the one she had given to her staff, things were only forty minutes behind. Her luck seemed to be holding—she located Mickey via the limousine phone and reshuffled the acts so his lateness would not make a big hole in the sequence. When he showed up, she personally threw him onstage.

"Does anything ever ruffle you, Ms. Chant?" her golden shadow asked. "You're as cool and still as a pond."

The praise made her warm, a much more pleasant warmth than the muggy heat that caused her own tank top to stick like plastic wrap. She caught a glimpse of herself in the tiny mirror of a cigarette machine and winced. The neat blond braid she had put into her hair that morning had become a rattail of fuzzy ends, her powder and blush had long since trickled down her neck, and she felt as grimy as the inside of a vacuum cleaner.

"I'd like to jump *into* a pond right now," she replied.

"Is it always this insane?"

Chris clearly wasn't a regular on the rock scene, she decided. No wonder she hadn't recognized him. Once seen, he would certainly have stuck in her mind like a burr; only brain damage would have dislodged him. "It's usually a bit worse, actually. We haven't had any *truly* horrible crises yet."

A piercing shriek told her she had spoken too soon. Lorelei, Chris and half a dozen other people dashed to the source of the cry—a dressing room crowded with people who shouldn't have been there. They milled uselessly around a young man stretched out on the floor, who was gasping and turning purple. Lorelei pushed herself through the unresisting crowd and knelt beside him. Oh, Lord, she thought, could she remember her CPR? Was it fifteen compressions to every two breaths? Chris appeared on the other side of the prone body, an oasis of calm and confidence. Seeming to know exactly what he was doing, he loosened the boy's collar and felt for a pulse in the neck. His steady eyes met Lorelei's. "He's breathing, and there's a strong pulse."

She started to calm down. The boy started to twitch.

Chris looked around at the people nearby. "Was he doing anything? Pills? Coke?"

A tearful girl answered, "No, he was just eating chili!" She sobbed.

Chris continued, patient but insistent. "Is he epileptic?"

"No."

"Does he have any allergies—to food or anything?"

She looked surprised. "Well, he said something once about being allergic to anchovies and peanuts, but . . ."

"That's probably it, then," he murmured to Lorelei. "Get a doctor. He's going into shock."

"Why?" she asked, reaching for her walkie-talkie.

"Some restaurants use peanut butter to thicken their chili."

She never doubted him for a moment, his manner was too assured. She depressed the walkie-talkie button. "Attention, everyone. We need the doctor and the crash cart in dressing room fourteen *stat*. Hear me? Send the doctor and cart to number fourteen." To cover all bases, she got up from the floor and scrambled for the telephone. The crowd parted before her. Even as she dialed the emergency number, the doctor and his nurse burst in with their equipment.

Lorelei stood to one side as they worked, getting even more comfort from Chris's presence than from that of the medical experts. He had done nothing elaborate, just taken a pulse, asked a couple of pertinent questions and decided on the proper action—exactly what you always hoped *someone* would do in a crisis.

"Chris, you want a job here?" she asked.

He watched the boy as he was carried out on a stretcher and answered with a firm "No."

Lorelei managed to laugh. Then her walkie-talkie buzzed with Gil's ragged voice. "Lorelei! What's this crap I'm hearing about a drug overdose in the dressing rooms? If you know anything about it, you'd better get up to the security office and file a report. I'm already dialing the insurance company."

Lorelei was astonished to see her hand shake as she operated the talk button. "Okay, Gil, I'm on my way."

In the dressing room, the spirits of the crowd had dimmed noticeably. People stood around looking stunned. Lorelei herself looked blankly at her clipboard and realized she hadn't the faintest idea where she was in her schedule. On her way to the security office she'd have to find one of her assistants to take over for a while. So intent was she on getting her professional bearings, she hardly noticed that Chris had maneuvered her out into a quiet side corridor.

"Was that the obligatory crisis?" he asked ironically.

"I *hope* so. I'm not sure how many more I can deal with, or let *you* deal with. You're good at this. Thank you."

He executed a small but gallant bow. "Just be happy there are Good Samaritan laws and that Gil probably has tons of insurance."

"*Insurance!*" she groaned. "I've got to get up the front gates before Gil goes all to pieces." She hurried toward the main corridor.

"I don't think it's such a good idea to run," Chris said sternly as he himself jogged to catch her.

Lorelei had begun to discover what he meant. The combination of heat, tension and the aftermath of crisis suddenly sucked everything out of her head and left a queasy gray haze. She put one hand out to the wall and stopped, willing herself to remain upright.

A moment later, to her mortification, she was in Chris's arms in a faint. Before her wits cleared, she had the serene sense of being utterly safe in his embrace, protected from all harm, free of all care—not an illusion a woman should indulge in, she warned herself. She shook it off determinedly, but Chris remained concerned.

"I'm okay, you can let me go," she assured him.

He did not. For an endless moment his eyes burned down into hers, coals of blue fire beneath the smoky bars of his eyebrows. She noticed irrelevantly that he had webs of tiny lines under his eyes. They looked as if the sun had baked them into the bronze of his skin. He smelled gorgeous, hot and vital and male.

Breaking the spell, he swept her off her unsteady feet and sat her down on a spool of electrical cable. "Head between your knees," he ordered unromantically.

Lorelei took one look at the stern set of his jaw and obeyed. "Really, I'm okay," she mumbled through the fabric of her jeans. "It's low blood pressure. I just grayed out for a second."

"My other patient was more cooperative."

"I'm being cooperative!" She sat up and glared.

He pushed her head back down. "Good. Then sit still. I'll be right back."

Even though he had left, she didn't dare disobey. She would have let the entire concert unravel rather than provoke her ad hoc doctor. She did, however, chance a look above her knees when she heard the hum of an electric golf cart. Chris had told her to sit, but not to get run over. The cart stopped just as she managed to focus on its driver...Chris. He hopped out and graciously helped her into the passenger seat; his eyes held a suspiciously self-satisfied gleam. Lorelei leaned back in the seat, glorying in the experience of being driven through the halls by such a stunning driver.

"I'm not even going to ask where you got this," she sighed. Then she noticed little pieces of memo paper stuck all over the dash and recognized the handwriting. "This is Gil's cart! You swiped this from Gil!"

"Well, it was just sitting there," he protested. "Waste not, want not—a motto I try to live and work by."

He drove carefully, coaxing his way through the crowds with politeness and charm. A few women nearly came to grief when they stood too long staring at him, but Lorelei told herself that that was hardly his fault. Women had to be wary of men like Chris, whether driving or otherwise.

"Just what work do you do, Mr. Christian? Not anything in rock, I take it."

"Not rock, although your field does seem to offer enough thrills and chills for anyone. No, I'm . . . a pilot."

"A test pilot? A pilot for the airlines? Air force?"

"None of the above. I fly a twin-engine Beechcraft Duchess for a private organization. I get enough excitement that way."

Lorelei indulged in a momentary vision of him, scarf streaming, in the open cockpit of a type of plane that had probably gone out of use with the Red Baron.

"Here you are, and that looks like the security chief himself coming to meet you."

Lorelei forced herself out of her pleasant reverie. Chris had somehow found his way up all the ramps and turns to the front of the stadium. He evidently had an infallible sense of direction—probably a good quality in a pilot, she allowed. With great reluctance she hopped out onto the hot concrete, shading her eyes against the strong light. He looked at home in the fierce sunshine, his tan glowed, and he had obviously gotten the fine lines around his eyes from squinting.

"I'll go return this cart," he remarked. "Can't let your boss walk like a normal mortal."

"God forbid." She put her hand on the fender of the cart to keep him there for another moment. "I'm sorry we haven't had a chance to talk yet. What was it you wanted, anyway?"

A bright but enigmatic smile lit his face as he shifted gears. "That's quite all right. I've found out exactly what I wanted to know." Then he backed away and drove off.

"What?" Lorelei said, but if he heard, he made no sign. The security chief reached her and cleared his throat. The cart had vanished around a concrete embankment, and Lorelei tore her eyes away.

Members of all the bands were onstage for the finale. Lorelei lay on one of the ratty old couches in the command center, clipboard on her stomach, telephone in one hand and walkie-talkie in the other. She watched the concert and the backstage activity on five TV monitors. Her helpers kept the door banging open and shut, but Gil had vanished upstairs to the VIP cocktail lounge. A small dark-haired girl wandered in.

"Hi, Sylvia," Lorelei greeted her. "How did you hold up back in New York?"

"Do you know how many telephone lines we have in that office?" the young girl asked wearily.

"Yeah, twenty-seven. And they were all ringing off the hook, right?"

"All day."

"I know, I've held down the home office during concerts before, too. Don't worry, you'll work the next one backstage—but you may not decide that it's much of an improvement." Breaking in a new assistant meant torturing them with work, but Sylvia, not quite out of her teens and usually as giddy as someone who had been breathing laughing gas, showed signs of surviving. Lorelei wondered if she herself, at twenty-four, still had the necessary youth and resilience for the job. During every unguarded moment of the evening, when she should have been anticipating possible disasters, her mind had floated back to impossibly sweet memories of one golden-blond man. He couldn't really have been there, she decided. She had to have dreamed anyone so attractive. If not, *why* had he come? Why had he followed her around? What had he meant by his parting comment: "I've found out exactly what I wanted to know?"

She shook her head clear and flipped one more page on the clipboard. "Okay, Sylvia, we've got about ten more minutes before all hell breaks loose again. Then we'll be gently prying VIPs out of the dressing rooms and the lounges and pouring them into their limousines. We should get out of here around 12:30, but there are so many extra people at this show it could be 3:00 a.m. or worse. I can't believe all the hangers-on I've seen parading around with backstage passes *I* never gave them."

"Oh, that reminds me," Sylvia said. "Did Mr. Jansen find you?"

Jansen? Lorelei fished for the name in the recesses of her memory. She found it linked to a charity organization called the Odin Foundation. "You mean the guy Gil is meeting tomorrow to talk about doing a benefit concert?"

"That's him—Chris Jansen."

Lorelei's heart began to beat a wild tattoo.

"He dropped by the office this afternoon and said he wanted to see how Gil ran a show. I told him it was more a case of how *you* ran a show and gave him one of the orange passes. Boy, is he a stunner! Did he find you?"

The exact circumstances in which he had found her, and everything that had followed, ran through Lorelei's mind at a nightmarish speed. "That was *him*?"

Her assistant looked perplexed.

"He never exactly said who he *was*, Sylvia! Oh, Lord . . . he saw Gil at his most obnoxious."

"There's no way to avoid that."

"He saw me scream at a reporter."

"You *have* to scream at some of them."

"He told me he was a *pilot*!" Lorelei cried in exasperation.

"He *is* a pilot. He told me he had just flown back to New York from Guatemala. What does this Odin Foundation do, anyway?"

Lorelei rubbed her suddenly aching temples. "It's an organization of doctors who go to developing countries and volunteer their medical skills. Odin has two planes, big jets. One is fitted out as an ophthalmological hospital and the other is for plastic surgery, I think." Of course, Lorelei thought, she now understood Chris's ease with medical emergencies.

"Boy, I wouldn't mind having Chris Jansen as *my* doctor," Sylvia murmured.

"He's not a doctor, he's the general director. The medical director is some other guy—John Ward."

"Well, still. I hope I did the right thing in giving him that pass. I figured you were the best advertisement we had. We'd be sunk if he met *Gil* first."

"It was a nice thought," Lorelei told her kindly. But inside she felt sick with doubt. He had claimed to have found out exactly what he wanted to know. *What?* That rock concerts were exercises in controlled disaster? That Gil Gilman was a sarcastic, ill-tempered man with bad taste in clothes? That Lorelei Chant passed out after crises?

She picked herself up and dragged Sylvia out into the erupting chaos of the concert's finale. Whatever Chris Jansen had found out, Gil would doubtless let her know soon enough.

"I really don't think Revolver is the right place to pre-

sent this proposal, Gil." In suggesting that one of his plans
had a flaw, Lorelei knew she was taking her life in her
hands. He always met clients and contacts at groovy hot
spots; he loved to saunter through a packed house of ultra-
trendy young people and be recognized as a somebody in
their world. But Lorelei knew by sure instinct that their
world was not Chris Jansen's.

"The Odin Foundation sounds like a conservative sort of
outfit," she tried. "You know, doctors with homes in
Scarsdale and kids on the country-club swim team."

"Look, Jansen's only thirty-five or forty years old. I
checked. There are plenty of rockers on the road older than
him."

"Yes, but..."

"But nothing. These Odin people *want* rock and roll, remember? The board of directors or trustees, or whoever
they are, contacted *me*, not vice versa. So if you're going
with me, you're going to have to *look* like you can do rock
and roll. Get me?" Had he waited for an answer, he
wouldn't have liked the one Lorelei wanted to give him.

At least she looked human again, and for that she offered up thanks. A night's sleep had done her a world of
good and the day's follow-up concert work hadn't been too
hard. Did she look like someone who could "do rock and
roll?" She would have to, she decided. She had no intention of racing to her Chelsea apartment and changing just
to uphold Gil's image. The red tube-knit dress would have
to do. In the office bathroom she brushed her hair into a
simple ponytail that swung to her waist and dug her earrings out of her pocketbook. The rich heavy gold of the
loops reminded her of Chris Jansen. Her cheeks flushed at
the thought, and she glared into the mirror more critically.
Were those freckles on her face? Drat, they were, and they
made her turned-up scrap of a nose look more as if it belonged on Huck Finn than ever. She had always had a
problem achieving the washed-out sophistication proper in

the world of rock. Her pale skin blushed and burned and popped out in freckles. Her swamp-green eyes looked wide and slightly surprised no matter how languid she tried to make them, and she had a mouth like a Kewpie doll's. Her only advantage lay in the fact that she was tall, slim and very leggy. Some people never even looked as far up as her face.

Gil waited for her on Sixth Avenue in front of their building. He was wearing his usual designer jogging suit. He mistakenly thought the style made him look vigorous and funky.

"Now remember," he growled in his harsh Bronx accent. "You're just keeping Jansen happy while I exchange a few words with the manager about that party on Friday. No business, understand? You leave the pitch to me."

Lorelei smoldered for a good part of the ride downtown, her thoughts like splashes of acid. She knew every detail of the Odin proposal. Indeed, she had taken some of Gil's vague ideas and turned them *into* details, but evidently he felt she couldn't be trusted to explain them to a client. She was supposed to shut up and be ornamental. Sometimes, she thought, working for Gil was like being beaten with a stick.

Little by little, the prospect of seeing Chris Jansen put her in a much more pleasant state of mind. She didn't like to remember that the last time he had seen her, the *only* time he had seen her, she had been drenched in sweat and stumbling with fatigue. Tonight would be her last chance to correct that. Certainly she would never see him again, since the possibility of a gentleman like Chris hiring a barbarian like Gil seemed small. He would most likely listen to Gil's pitch with apparent interest, shake his hand politely and go elsewhere.

It was too early for Revolver to be busy; the in crowd usually bopped in around 9:00 p.m., stoking themselves with dinner before they hit the dance clubs. Now, at 6:00 p.m., the only customers were tourists who had wandered in by chance and business people from the surround-

ing Greenwich Village area. Gil left Lorelei at the door and
barged into the manager's office as if he owned it.

The spiky-haired hostess gave Lorelei a bored smile.
"Two of you for dinner?"

"Actually, my boss and I are meeting someone. . ." She
peered into the deep gloom of the long bar that led toward
the dining room. "In fact, there he is." Although Chris's
sleek charcoal-gray suit blended in with the shadows, his
unmistakable figure seemed to glow with its own light. A
drink sat untouched in front of him. He stood quietly, not
smoking, not fidgeting, more totally comfortable and un-
self-conscious in his own skin than anyone Lorelei had ever
seen.

The hostess followed her line of sight to Chris, then muttered in a tone of awe, "Lucky girl!"

At that moment, Chris's gaze swept to the front of the
restaurant and settled on Lorelei. He smiled, and she felt as
if she had just won the lottery. Leaving his drink, he made
his way up to her in lazy, graceful strides. She could see the
pilot in him—he had a certain longsighted look, the alert but
easy confidence of a man who routinely put thousands of
feet between himself and solid ground. But he didn't swag-
ger, she noticed, unlike some twenty-five-year-old fighter
jock. He was far too cool for that. Lorelei smiled as he approached, hoping she didn't have a foolish expression on her
face. She had met nearly every major star in rock, from fa-
bled veterans to the blazing new kids, but none had prepared her for the effect Chris had on her.

"Glad to see you lived through the concert." His voice
was as deep and craggy as a canyon.

Lorelei feigned hurt. "Did you doubt it?"

"Not for a moment." He signaled the hostess, who was
hovering over him shamelessly. The girl's eyes grew dewy
with pleasure, and she leaped to lead them to a table. When
they had been seated, Lorelei found herself destroyed by

nervousness. "Gil will be along shortly," she said, fidgeting.

"That's all right. If someone has to tell me how rock and roll is going to solve all my problems, I'd rather it be you. I might actually *believe* you."

She was suddenly grateful she had been forbidden to do the pitch. Her suspicions had been well-founded—this man was not buying. "Sorry, can't steal my boss's thunder. He'll explain it."

"What are you, then? Window dressing?"

"Something like that. I'm supposed to keep you entertained so you won't notice he's late. How am I doing?"

She had handed him the perfect opening for a comic reply. Instead, he leaned back and gave her a searching, troubled look. "How old are you?"

"I'm legal." The words popped out before she could consider how they might sound. "I mean, I'm twenty-four." Just barely, she added to herself.

He dragged his fingers through his tawny mane. It was the first nervous habit she had witnessed. "Hell, I had my pilot's license before you were walking."

Lorelei did some quick calculations. If one could fly at sixteen, he must be thirty-seven or thirty-eight. A generation in rock could be as short as three or four years. She felt unexpectedly young and raw. She changed the subject. "Why didn't you tell me who you were at the stadium?"

"I apologize for that." His blue eyes softened with an earnest light. "And I *did* tell you who I was, in a way. If we had met in any other circumstances, I would still have told you I was a pilot. That's how I think of myself. The stuff about Odin occurs to me later."

"A very neat excuse. But in actual fact you were spying."

"I was spying."

"And what did you discover?"

"That Lorelei Chant is an exceptionally capable field marshal who could pull off a very good benefit concert."

Something hung fire in his sentence. *"But?"*

"But, I'm not too convinced about the *benefits* of a benefit rock concert."

"Gil can make you a lot of money," she said staunchly.

"There's more to life than money." Chris looked chagrined. "I can't believe I just said that to someone I'm talking to about fund-raising."

She patted his arm comfortingly; the heavy swell of his muscles beneath the soft gray fabric gave her a deep pleasure. "We'll forget it happened."

The bandy-legged, gold-chain-draped figure of her boss popped out of the gloom like a poisonous mushroom. "Well, I see you two are getting along. Glad to meet you finally, Jansen. Sorry about the delay. You know how it is handling a big business—you're running all the time." He dragged out a chair, sat and helped himself to a bread stick. "You can split, Lori. Take the night off."

Lorelei had been expecting something like this, but she felt Chris tense like a cat about to spring. She tried to put calm and reassurance into her goodbye, but Chris bought none of it. As soon as she stood up, he stood up as well. Gil looked perplexed at being left at knee level.

"I'll see you to the door, Ms. Chant."

"Oh, that's not necessary."

"Yes, it is." A thin smile lightened Chris's thunderous look. "A kid your age shouldn't be standing out in front of a place like this all alone."

His small flash of humor lasted only until they reached the sidewalk. She put out her hand to hail a cab, and he pulled her back. His grip felt angry, and she met his eyes apprehensively.

"Window dressing is okay once in a while, Lorelei," he growled. "Doormat is another story."

"I don't get my self-image from him, I just work for him. He's very good at what he does."

"Yeah, he's got creep down to a fine art."

"Tell me, Chris, how did your trustees come up with the idea of holding a rock concert?"

He rubbed his hands over his face in distress. "Oh, lord! I don't know—spontaneous mass hysteria?"

"But you're going through the motions of looking for a producer anyway?"

"I'm considering proposals." Seeing her skeptical look, he added, "I *am*, really. I'm a reasonable man. I'd never turn down a *good* idea."

"Then you will give Gil's idea a chance?"

"I *should* just leave now and stick him with the check, but since we haven't ordered anything, it wouldn't be much of a gesture."

"Just give him an hour."

"All right, one hour." His eyes twinkled in the long light of the summer evening. "But there are other people I'd rather give it to."

Flustered, she nearly fell into the taxi that stopped for her. Chris leaned in the window and gave her a last cockeyed grin. "Are you sure you're legal?"

She was unable to frame the slightest reply. He backed away, and the taxi drove off.

Chapter Two

Chris gave Lorelei's boss the promised hour; then he escaped the abrasive little man's company and went for a walk in order to think. He knew he was in trouble even before he found himself by the Metropolitan Museum, eighty blocks north. He hadn't spent a single block of his four-mile hike thinking about Gilman's proposal; he had spent it thinking about Gilman's assistant. Something about her sounded every alarm in his head. No one had rattled him so in eight years, not since he had met John Ward and found himself involved in Odin. Until then, Chris had never let a job or a woman become more important than his freedom. Jobs were ways to keep flying. Women were fun. Odin made up for its demands on him by returning a deep satisfaction that he had never expected, but that was no guarantee that a woman would ever do the same. Women were much more difficult to manage than jobs.

When he thought about it, he admitted his attitude toward women might be considered rather cavalier, but he didn't think it was. He liked them and they seemed to like him. As long as neither party expected more than the other was willing to give, his relationships always managed to be pleasant—or had, up to now. With Lorelei, he knew instinctively that the old equation would never balance. She had done nothing overt to suggest this. Despite her stunning jade-green eyes, she had never so much as cast him a flirtatious look. It was his own reaction to her that threw him off.

He had met more beautiful women, as well as women who had made more aggressive *use* of their beauty, but he had never met anyone so appealing. After seeing Lorelei cool and collected at the restaurant, he knew she *could* achieve the fine gloss of a fashion layout if she so desired. But he had also seen her, and frankly preferred her, with her fabulous ash-blond hair flying like a mare's tail and perspiration trickling down her slender neck. She had the type of bred-in-the-bone beauty that could neither be applied with makeup nor rubbed off. And she had absolutely no idea of it! She was all caught up in her crazy job, and her earnestness made her even *more* appealing to Chris. She took on situations no sane person would touch and made them seem like business as usual. Given a little background, she could probably even run one of Odin's missions.

She was a beautiful woman and one he could admire; Chris could not afford to face the combination. He thanked God she was fourteen years younger than he and from a different world. After he formally turned down her slimy boss's unworkable plan, they would never run across each other again. All he had to do was behave in a sane manner until then.

One look at her boss the next morning confirmed Lorelei's suspicions—the hour with Chris had not gone well. Gil's wiry hair was bunched in clumps like rusty steel wool, his eyes shone red as beets, and nothing pleased him, from the music on the radio to the amount of cream cheese on the bagel she brought him. Sylvia and the other employees hid in the outer office.

"Who does Jansen think he is, anyway? Mother Teresa? St. Joan? What...is he divinely inspired or something?"

"Have some decaffeinated coffee, Gil." Lorelei felt a twinge of guilt. She had passed the night in extraordinarily sweet dreams that had featured the divinely inspired Chris Jansen. "Did he pinpoint what was wrong with the plan?"

"Pinpoint? He blasted them with TNT! He says a stadium concert is unmanageable, his message will get lost. He says merchandising with T-shirts and buttons and stuff is tacky. He says the bands I've got lined up don't present the right image for Odin. He doesn't want a concert, he wants a visitation from the ghost of Albert Schweitzer!"

Lorelei sputtered into her own coffee until Gil glared at her. Recovering fast, she switched to a bland look.

"You sure you didn't sour him on the deal last night?" Gil's small eyes shrank to mean black pebbles of suspicion. "Now that I think of it, you two seemed awful chummy by the time I got to you. What were you talking about, anyway?"

"You didn't leave us much *to* talk about. First you tell me not to talk about business with him and then you tell me I'm too *chummy*. What was I supposed to do, talk about the weather for twenty minutes?"

"Keep pushing, Miss Smartmouth. You think you can run a business like this yourself? I'd like to see you try. You've been getting a free ride on my name so long you think you're a big wheel now. I ought to fire you just to show you what a nobody you still are."

She waited, but he didn't fire her. He merely raged while she silently counted to one hundred over and over. One day he really would fire her, as he had fired every other assistant he had ever had. Three years earlier, when she'd started the job, industry people had predicted she'd last six months. Now someone called her every couple of weeks with a job offer—tour manager, publicity director, events organizer. One day she would say yes to one of them and leave Gil flat.

For now, she decided, she'd at least see this thing through with Chris Jansen. There existed the tiniest possibility that he *would* hire Gil.

She believed in that possibility only until lunchtime, which, as usual for Lorelei, came closer to three o'clock than noon. She left Sylvia to handle the telephones and flung herself out into the hot glare of midtown Manhattan. The murderous noise of the traffic and the indiscriminate buffeting of the crowds seemed easier to take than Gil's moods. She bought a falafel from a vendor and sat down on the ledge of one of the fountains that lined Sixth Avenue. She opened up the new issue of Billboard magazine and saw a long article on the Giants Stadium concert. Her name was correctly spelled, and a photo showed her with two of the bands. Ha! she thought. Gil could make all the dire pronouncements he wished about her place in the industry, but Billboard seemed to know who she was.

"Not a bad picture," said a deep voice somewhere off to the right above her shoulder.

Lorelei glanced up and found Chris Jansen standing there in the brilliant sunshine. The light flared out around him in a very fitting corona. He was eating an ice-cream cone—pistachio, she thought. The color matched his pale aqua-blue suit.

"Want a bite?" He sat cheerfully on the ledge beside her with no apparent concern for the safety of his trousers.

"No, thank you. I'm exactly one bite of ice cream away from not fitting into my clothes."

"Get new clothes. Clothes should always suit your life-style, after all. And ice cream is an indispensable part of a civilized life-style. Some wise man said that."

"I'm sure. Well, tell him there's no such thing as being too thin in rock—and I work in rock, remember?"

He cas* a disapproving glance up the block at Radio City Music Hall. According to its marquee, a rock band was performing there that night. "Yeah, I seem to be having trouble forgetting that."

Lorelei didn't have enough nerve to ask him what he meant. She changed the subject. "I didn't think Odin had an office in the city. Do you live here or just come in for the ice cream?"

"Neither. I live upstate in an itty-bitty town called Teeterbrouck. It has an airport where I can keep the airplane and avoid the traffic jams at the big metropolitan airports. The Odin office is at my house. I'm here on business. I just walked out of that building behind us with a check for fifty thousand dollars—for Odin, of course. And then I saw you. It must be my lucky day."

She decided to take his charm at face value. It was so pleasant sitting with him in the clear sunlight that she wanted nothing to dim it. "Tell me, is it true what I read in the Odin annual report, that you got the idea for the foundation eight years ago in an Argentinian bar?"

He grimaced. "Yeah, I'm afraid so. You know how many empires are built in bars...I've built *my* share of them. Most don't last through the next morning's hangover. But this time I was shooting the breeze with a very unusual fellow. He said he had been head of surgery at a big New York City hospital, but had retired early to do two years in the Peace Corps. His stint was over, and he was traveling around before going back home."

"That was John Ward?" she asked, picturing the name on the Odin letterhead.

"Right. Pretty weird thing for a sixty-year-old man to be doing, I thought, but you don't question the backgrounds of the gringos you meet in Argentinian bars."

"I'm sure you don't," she agreed. What background had brought the thirty-year-old *Chris* to that bar? she wondered.

"He and I drank shot after shot of tequila and thrashed out this big plan to save the world. He had the medical angles, I figured out how to put it in the air. I really *am* a pilot, you know.

"In the morning he found me again and gave me his card. Said he was serious about the idea we had cooked up and for me to contact him when I got back to the States. Of course, at that point I figured if I was ever going to see the U.S. again, they'd have to ship it to me parcel post."

"What were you doing in Argentina that was so great?" She waited tensely for news of a beloved *señorita*, or even a wife and kids.

"I was flying fire patrols and roundups for cattle ranchers on the pampas."

"Oh. That sounds . . . interesting."

He laughed in delight. "If you like flying, it's heaven. But I guess Johnny's talk was eating at me. A month later I switched to flying an air ambulance, and a while after that I found myself right here in New York, chatting up the rich folks who became Odin's first backers. The rest, as they say, is history."

"The seed of altruism really took root, huh?"

"Egad." He winced. "Don't spread that around. How about you? How'd you get into the rock and roll circus?"

"You mean a nice girl like me? I was born into it. I'm just following in the old man's footsteps—he owned a nightclub that he turned into a rock club when my sister and I were teenagers. He said he wanted to know where we were when we went out at night, so we might as well be at our own club. He had a little more influence on us than he planned, I think."

Chris seemed to enjoy her story immensely. "Remind me that when I have a little girl I'd better not teach her to *fly* just so I can know where *she* is."

The idea of Chris having a little girl pleased Lorelei immensely. What a great father he would make, she thought.

He seemed so easygoing and funny and warm. Actually, he'd make a good anything: boss, partner, friend, husband— She cut off the thought abruptly.

"What does your sister do?" he asked.

"She's a singer. Oops, I'm not supposed to say that anymore. She's made several albums, country rock, I guess you'd call it. She has a good-sized following, but she's determined to make the big crossover to acting. Right now she's finishing up a movie in east Africa."

His eyes sparkled with interest, and Lorelei felt a stab of unreasonable jealousy toward her own sister. She knew from the pamphlets that Odin had flown missions to east Africa. *Rosie* should be here talking to Chris—they'd have a lot to talk about. He probably found Lorelei's all-consuming interest in rock boring. He might have no use for rock at all, unless he played it on his airplane's radio.

"Why such a scowl, Lorelei Chant?" Chris had gently pinched her chin and brought her face around to his. "Is it something about your sister?"

His eyes were so beautiful, she thought. Their deep setting turned them into triangles fringed by caramel-colored lashes. "No . . . no, I'm just feeling guilty about sitting here having a nice chat on my boss's time. I ought to be cultivating your business." Chris's sigh and the sudden distance in his eyes confirmed her fears. "I take it Gil's proposal leaves you unsatisfied on several points?"

"Charmingly put, Ms. Chant." His cheeks crinkled with a brief smile.

"Could it be changed to suit you?"

"I really don't think a Gil Gilman plan could be changed *enough*."

It took every last shred of her employee loyalty to keep Lorelei from agreeing.

"It's not rock that's the problem, Lorelei. Well, maybe it is. I *like* the idea of getting kids and young people excited about the world and solving its problems. They can have such great enthusiasm. But their attention spans are so *short*."

"Just like the public's in general."

"That's true, unfortunately. It's hard to keep people interested in a problem that won't go away. I don't make the mistake of thinking Odin is solving anything on a big scale. Huge organizations like CARE and UNESCO are floundering. Odin is just a bandage. We spend five million dollars a year running the two jets on maybe six or seven missions each. Depending on the length of each stay, we operate on one to three hundred people per trip. Hopefully we pass on a few techniques to the doctors in the host countries so they can continue with the work themselves. Now, it's enough for *me* that some little girl is able to smile because our surgeon fixed a birth defect, but it's not going to make a huge impact on the world situation."

"You don't make any grandiose claims like that in your literature."

"No, but...people sort of *expect* it once you become a big-name cause. They get all this feverish excitement built up, and they work very hard. During the event there's a tremendous outpouring of concern and human kindness. And then a month later the problem is still there. A year later it's *still* there and the people who supported you are discouraged."

"So you need to educate them a little more."

He gave her a frank look tinged with his warm, rich humor. "Do you see your boss as a great educator?"

"Ugh." She frowned. "Okay, you need sponsors who understand that they're going to be pouring money into you from now until...well, for quite a while. You need sponsors who will *regularly* hand you fifty-thousand-dollar checks."

He nodded for her to go on.

"Sounds like corporate sponsors, foundations, federal money."

"No government money, it's too politically loaded."

"Okay, skip the government." She put her brain to work, aware that he seemed to be enjoying the progress of her thoughts. "Since your trustees have had this little attack of desperation about a rock concert, I take it the problem is Odin's low profile. You can't attract the big money until you make it into the public eye. You've got to glamorize Odin somehow, get the interest of the people with the big money." The conclusion was obvious and discouraging. "A rock concert is going after the wrong audience." She began to curl the end of her braid around her fingers; it was a habit born of frustration. "Do you want me to explain this to Gil?"

"Good heavens, no! You've got enough on your plate just being civil to the man. I'll do my own dirty work. I just…" His voice dropped to an earnest rumble. "I know I wasn't very up-front with you at the start—at Giants Stadium—so I want to be sure you understand my decision. It's got nothing to do with personalities. You're more than enough to make up for Gil."

She couldn't keep the surprise out of her face, or the flush of pleasure. She told herself he didn't mean it as profoundly as she wanted to believe, but even a bit of Chris Jansen's regard would warm her for days.

"And I know you're competent," he continued. "If you worked for somebody we could actually use, I know the project would be a success."

"You be careful what declarations you throw around, Mr. Jansen. You never know when you'll have to make good on one." Successfully breaking the serious mood he had cast, she stood up. Chris rose with her, the shadow of a frown darkening his tanned brow. "Thank you for the explanation, Chris…and for the warning. I'll make sure I'm out of the office when you talk to Gil."

"I guess I'll go up and see him now. No sense in letting this drag on." To his credit, as low as his opinion was of Gil, he showed no enthusiasm for the task.

"In that case, I'll go get myself an ice-cream cone, maybe even a sundae—it'll take longer to eat." She held out her hand, amazed she was able to face so steadily the end of her time with Chris Jansen. "I'm sorry I won't be working for you, Chris. I know you don't hang out at rock concerts as a rule, but if you ever find yourself at another one of mine, come backstage and say hello. I'll probably be able to put you to work again."

"I'll be all yours." His grip on her hand was too sweet, too personal to bear. She tugged her fingers away as quickly as she could without seeming abrupt, then made herself jump into the street to catch the Walk light. She remembered not to turn toward her building, since Chris would be heading there to lower the boom on Gil. She continued east past Radio City, through the tourist-choked complex of Rockefeller Center and onto Fifth Avenue. After that, she paid no attention to where her feet fell. Her mind was too busy. What was she supposed to think about Chris Jansen? Only a very special man would have taken the time to talk to her as he had, a considerate, sensitive man. Any other potential client would have called Gil on the phone, expressed the standard regrets that the proposal didn't suit them and left it at that. There would have been no tender concern for the poor underlings who would bear the brunt of Gil's fury or who might wonder what had gone wrong.

Unfortunately, Chris's touching regard for her feelings wasn't enough. The Fates had thrown her a real curve—they had showed her Chris Jansen and snatched him away again. Ignorance would have been so much easier to bear.

"What a sour puss you have on your face! This is the welcome I get after five months in darkest Africa?"

Lorelei nearly dropped the satchel of personal belongings she had just dragged home from the office. An older, tanner, auburn-haired woman with a pug nose and high cheekbones identical to her own stood in the middle of Lorelei's small Chelsea apartment holding a glass of bourbon. "Rosie!" Lorelei threw down the bag, let the door slam and flew into her sister's arms. "You're still supposed to be in Kenya!"

"We wrapped up the shooting early. Can you believe it? Max is the only director in the known world who comes in ahead of schedule, though *not* under budget. I was going to spend a week or two shopping in London before I came back, but I missed my baby sister."

"Yeah, sure. What man are you currently chasing who lives in New York?"

Rosie pouted. "Meanie! If I was after a man, wouldn't I have gone to *his* place? Instead I'm here to cheer you up as you fall in the door. You're a mess, honey. What has Gil the Pill been dumping on you lately?"

"The usual," Lorelei mumbled.

"Here, let me take that bag and pour you some of your own bourbon. Lord, what have you got in here? It weighs as much as one of my suitcases."

It should, Lorelei commented to herself. It held the three years' worth of knickknacks that had accumulated on her desk.

But Rosie gave her no time to answer. "How are you getting on with that poor imitation of human life you call your boss?"

"Oh," Lorelei said weakly. "No problems anymore."

Rosie turned around from the counter where she had been cracking a tray of ice. "Anymore? That sounds morbid. Did somebody finally take out a contract on him?"

"No, I'm afraid he's still alive and kicking."

"Then what, honey?" Rosie's mouth formed an O. "Lorelei, you didn't get fired, did you?"

Her answer was firm. "I'm very certain I quit first."

"Well, it's about time! Here, you *need* a drink. When did all this happen?"

"About an hour ago." Lorelei took the drink. She didn't need it to calm her nerves; she needed it to celebrate. She had been in shock the whole taxi ride home but felt it lifting now, leaving not a post-disaster depression but light-hearted joy. "I really did it, Rosie. I'm finally free of that man!"

"Well, now, I did get home on a momentous occasion. Sit down and tell me all about it. Whatever made my stoic little sister finally get fed up?"

"Oh, Gil was just blaming me after a client rejected one of his proposals. Saying ridiculous things like...well, he didn't make sense, you know? He was just making up accusations as they occurred to him. First he claimed I had said the wrong things, treated Chris wrong—"

"Chris?"

"The client," Lorelei corrected hastily. "Chris Jansen. Then he decided that I wasn't just inept, I had *motives* for making Chris—Mr. Jansen—dump the proposal."

"*Motives?* Like what? To steal him for yourself? Strike out on your own?"

"Yeah, exactly. You're good at this, Rosie. You could go at it professionally."

"So could you."

"Huh?"

"I don't mean analyzing bosses, I mean producing concerts. You're free now. So *steal* this Jansen guy. Go into business for yourself. Ah, now *that's* got you thinking."

Indeed it had. Lorelei had always assumed she'd need a long apprenticeship before she could do anything so bold as become an independent. But weren't three years with Gil the equal—in experience as well as wear and tear—of ten with anyone else? Slow down, she told herself. The thought of having Chris as her own client was undoubtedly clouding her judgment.

"The client doesn't want a rock concert, Rosie. He was very firm."

Her sister shrugged. "So? Who says you have to give him a rock concert? Give him whatever the heck he wants. If there's one thing I found out doing that movie, it's that producing a film is very much like producing a record or a concert tour. It's just a big mess that needs to be organized and run by a despot. That's you."

"Oh, thanks."

"Well, okay, you're a benevolent despot, but when you say 'jump,' honey, people get high off the ground. I've seen it."

Not sure whether to be flattered or piqued, Lorelei obeyed her sister's offhand gesture and fetched the bourbon bottle. "Some despot *I* am, running at *your* every whim."

"Who do you think *trained* you? Listen, I'm going to say this one more time and then I'm going to let you make your own remarkably astute decisions. If you want to go solo, do it. I'll back you every step of the way. And it's just a guess, but since you already have a head start in thinking about what this Jansen fellow wants, don't write him off just because he's dumped Gil. It just means he's got good sense. So that's all the sisterly wisdom I'm going to lay on you. Come here and ask me about Africa."

Rosie did not quite keep her promise to let Lorelei make her own decisions. She took an apartment in a neighborhood she considered funky enough for a rising movie star, bought a silver Mercedes and nagged her younger sister all through the winter....

"Why are you running some little theater festival in Danbury?" she demanded when Lorelei took the job. "You should be doing something big and important."

Two months later it was "What do you mean the Kansas City Arts Council has hired you to organize its February lecture series? That doesn't mean you have to go to *Kansas*, does it?"

Finally Lorelei took a job that almost met her sister's approval. "Well, okay, road-managing a rock tour at least makes sense, but you're not going to be out of town *long*, are you?"

Lorelei put up with all this loving criticism as she had always put up with the much less loving criticism from Gil. No matter how deep the oceans of confidence Rosie might have had in her, Lorelei knew there was more to becoming an independent producer than a brash manner. She wanted to get out of rock, or at least be qualified to get out of it if the opportunity came along. Since losing the Odin job—Chris's job—her association with rock music had seemed like a real rock—around her ankles. She knew she wouldn't always be twenty-four years old, and she had no intention of becoming an aging hanger-on like Gil, looking to kids half her age for acceptance. She had always *liked* other forms of entertainment and she could very well learn to produce them.

"You of all people ought to understand, Rosie!" Lorelei complained. She had met her sister at a posh hotel overlooking Central Park South. Outside, the traffic splashed through gray end-of-the-winter slush. Inside, amid towering floral arrangements, ladies draped their furs over the backs of Louis Quinze chairs and talked about galas. Lorelei felt sure she had been let in by mistake.

"Look at this place, Rosie. Back in the old days of Rosie the Rocker you'd never have been caught dead drinking espresso with the Rockefellers. *You* want to shrug off your disreputable past, too. This man of yours must really have you going."

Her sister looked guiltily at the skirt of the tasteful angora dress she had worn.

Lorelei pressed her point. "I know you. You're getting in practice for when you're a celebrated movie star. Speaking of which, have they finally decided on a title for this flick?"

"*The Veldt*," Rosie answered glumly.

"That's a good title. What's wrong?"

"The promotion. I'm going to be back on the road with a guitar and a bottle of beer if somebody doesn't light a fire under the promotion department at Pioneer Films." She started to twist the strands of her pearls. "Oh, Lorelei, it's dull, dull, dull! The same old routine they use with every movie—a couple of full-page ads, screenings for the critics, me on a few talk shows. This is a classy film. It's based on a Pulitzer Prize-winning novel, for gosh sake! And it's a terrific love story, it could be the hit of the next season."

"Well, I suppose it's like record albums. The company puts out too many to give each one the push it deserves. I wish you were still singing. I could take you out on the road and promote up a storm." After Lorelei finished saying that, she decided she didn't at all like the sly look that had crept into her sister's face.

"I was hoping you'd come up with that idea."

"What idea?"

"Promoting my film."

"Promoting your... Now, Rosie, I said nothing of the sort. I—"

"You *are* 'between projects,' to put it politely, correct? Actually, you don't have *anything* lined up for the future, do you? Well, why not do this? Daddy always said we had to look out for one another. This is just what he meant. You'd be helping launch my career, and I'd be helping launch yours, sort of. Oh, think about it, Lorelei! Think about it before you say no, give it an hour!"

The phrase hooked into something deep in Lorelei's memory. Many months ago she had begged Chris Jansen to give Gil's proposal an hour. Her mind swirled again with thoughts of Odin's director. No matter how busy she had kept herself since summer, it had never taken much to trigger these thoughts. Every time she picked up a trade paper she looked to see if Odin had finally announced its event. Now she understood why—in her heart she still considered Odin, and its director, to be hers.

"Lorelei? Lorelei! Don't leave me sitting here breathing on the crystal while you daydream. Have you got an idea for my movie or not?"

Lorelei didn't dare say what she was thinking, but she did smile.

Chapter Three

Chris swung his battered white Alfa Romeo through the Saturday-morning quiet of Teeterbrouck. After eight years as a bona fide resident, he no longer noticed what a contrast he made to his neighbors in their sleek new BMWs and Audis. When he thought about anything other than Odin, it was how strangely comfortable he felt owning a house and living in one place for so long he knew the shopkeepers by name. The old Chris Jansen would have been appalled.

This cold spring morning his thoughts were far less cozy. His head had been in an uproar since the telephone call on Friday. Unsuspecting, he had picked up the phone in the office annex of his house and heard the quiet, husky voice of Lorelei Chant. She had asked him, in her delightfully blunt way, if he would like to see a movie with her.

"Is this a date?" he had teased, knowing very well it wasn't. Her reply had been flustered until he'd put her at ease. But after agreeing to meet her at, of all places, Teeterbrouck's own movie theater, he had felt a small sense of letdown. He would have *liked* it to be a date, to think that she considered him dateworthy.

He had brusquely ordered himself to be reasonable. Months ago he had fought a pitched battle with his heart, and he had won. He couldn't throw away that victory today; Lorelei Chant was a dangerous woman for him to know. She pleased him on too many levels. When he let her into his mind at all, she galloped away with his wits. He did not need to become obsessed with a baby rock entrepreneur. He felt like a fool even considering it—an old fool.

Which didn't mean, however, that he had the guts to pass up a chance to see her again.

He saw her now, up ahead. She was standing beneath the peeling marquee of the Teeterbrouck Cinema, wearing a bright yellow-and-black plaid coat. She looked like a beacon light on some foggy coast, even more out of place in the reserved little Hudson Valley town than Chris. With her in mind, he had opted not to wear his usual Saturday-morning shredded jeans. His casual blue suit and open-collared white shirt was hardly flamboyant, but the girl at the gas station had given him a favorable glance.

He pulled up to the empty curb in front of the theater, fervently glad he didn't have to do any tricky parallel parking; the sight of Lorelei's sunflower-bright figure took all his attention. God, she was beautiful! he thought—even when all he could see of her were long, silky legs and a waterfall of frozen daiquiri-colored hair. Perhaps he shouldn't have come after all....

As he stepped out of the car, he covered his doubts with a crooked smile. "*Kiss of the Zombie?*"

"What?" Eyes like Chinese jade opened wide, mottled green jewels set in the gold of her lashes.

Chris shoved his hands deep into his pocket to keep from reaching out to touch her. He gestured awkwardly with his chin up to the marquee. "Is that the movie you wanted to see?"

She looked flustered for another moment, then recovered as she always seemed to recover. "How are you with blood?"

"Not very good."

"Then we'll have to see the film *I* brought."

Only then did Chris notice that she had two cases with her—a very businesslike attaché case and another one large enough to hold film reels. All possibility disappeared that this was a social meeting. Chris didn't know whether to be relieved or not. "You buying the popcorn?" he asked.

It was too early for popcorn. The concession stand lay dark, as did much of the musty old theater. A teenager with a broom let them in. Chris looked around, feeling odd to have the run of his own hometown theater. "How did you manage this?"

"Connections," Lorelei replied mysteriously.

"I hope Gil Gilman isn't saving us the aisle seats."

"What do you think?"

"That this isn't quite your boss's style."

"Ex-boss."

"What?" As he gazed at her in surprise, her sharp little chin rose proudly and a smile curved her lovely pink mouth. "Well, good for you! What happened? Or can I guess?"

She looked away—not from embarrassment, he decided, from integrity. She had never criticized her boss when she had worked for him and she wouldn't now. "We...had a disagreement. So I quit and he fired me. Now I'm an independent producer."

He stopped dead in the middle of the dim old lobby. "Does that mean you're thinking about making your own proposal to Odin?"

"Well, I've been keeping my eye on the trade papers, and I've noticed that you haven't hired anyone *else*. Your trustees haven't given up the idea, have they?"

I should be so lucky, Chris groaned to himself. In the eight months since he had turned down Gilman, he had turned down seven proposals from other producers. He spent what he considered an unreasonable amount of time explaining to his trustees why telethons and circuses would do little for Odin's image. They were ready to kill him.

"No," he grumbled, "they haven't given up the idea."

A soft touch on his arm cut through his funk. Lorelei's smile was sweet and sympathetic. "What about you?"

He couldn't think clearly until she took her hand away. "I told you, I'd never turn down an idea that made sense."

"Good. Then come along and see this movie." She rapped upon a door marked Manager and called softly, "We're ready, Mr. Macchio."

Chris resigned himself to seeing her movie.

When it was over, he admitted that there were more unpleasant ways to spend a morning. *The Veldt* was very good, a romantic adventure story set in a part of Africa he knew firsthand. When the film wasn't developing the tension between the heroine and her love interest, it managed to present a moving view of the hard lives of the local people.

There was something familiar about the gritty actress in the lead role. Rosie Champlain—the name meant nothing to him, but the face . . . He looked over at his hostess. The light from the screen played over her delicate features as the credits rolled, making him wonder how he had kept from putting an arm around her during the film. She and this Rosie Champlain could have been sisters, they looked so much alike. Memory stirred . . .

"Your sister is quite an actress."

She looked surprised. "You remembered!"

"You'd be amazed at how much I remember." Now what had he meant by that? he wondered. "Is Champlain her stage name?"

"Married name—ex-married name. She kept it for her singing career because she thought it sounded more country." Lorelei looked nervously at her fingers interlaced in her lap. "You don't think this is just another rock-singer-turns-actor movie, do you?"

"No. It's good. She's good. Of course, I'm a little disappointed we didn't see *Kiss of the Zombie*, but…" He felt her relax. "So what does *The Veldt* have to do with me, or with Odin?"

The theater manager interrupted them by yelling down from the top of the aisle, "Sorry to rush you out, Miss Chant, but we've got to get ready for the one o'clock show."

Chris waited in the lobby while Lorelei collected her heavy reels of film; then he carried them out for her and locked them in the trunk of her car, a Mercedes. "My sister's," she explained self-consciously.

The sun had burned off the morning fog. Teeterbrouck's gingerbread-trimmed Victorian buildings sparkled in the sunshine. People rambled up and down the sidewalks, pushing strollers and loading bags of groceries into station wagons. Chris waved to several of them and wondered avidly what they thought of the lovely woman at his side. He had rarely, if ever, strolled through the streets of his hometown with a woman of any sort.

Since leaving the theater, Lorelei had seemed to be at a loss. Chris took pity on her. "Okay, since I got cheated out of my popcorn, why don't you take me to brunch and tell me what's on your mind?"

Lorelei promptly agreed.

They ended up in the dining room of a boat club overlooking the Hudson River. The huge room gave them plenty of privacy for their discussion, but Lorelei still looked apprehensive. Chris struck a light note. "Whenever I eat here I think of all the billion-dollar deals that must have been closed in this very room." On second thought, maybe he had chosen the wrong note.

"Billion-dollar deals?"

"Sure, Teeterbrouck is one of the ritziest New York suburbs. All kinds of corporate heavyweights hang out here—

I've made a pitch or two myself over the crabmeat salad.''
He decided the time had come to get serious. "Are you here
with any billion-dollar deals, Lorelei?"

"Well, I'm definitely here to make a pitch, as I'm sure
you've figured out." She took a deep breath. "The movie
studio, Pioneer Films, thinks *The Veldt* is their best shot at
an Academy Award this year, and they don't want it to get
lost in the pack. It's sort of a quiet picture, a quality film,
you know? They've hired me to do something special to
promote it."

Icy fingers seemed to skate over his skin. "Something like
what?"

"I want to do the U.S. premiere as a benefit for Odin."
She flinched as if expecting a violent reaction from him.

"That's it?"

"No, not all of it. There's quite a bit more, actually." She
unlatched her briefcase and pulled out a neat black presentation folder with Odin Foundation—*The Veldt* Proposal
stamped in gold. "The premiere is just the central event, but
frankly there's not much money to be made for you there,
even though Pioneer has agreed to donate a nice percent-
age of the box-office receipts to the foundation.

"My plan is to send Rosie and a camera crew on one of
your missions and, from their footage, put together several
promotional spots and a documentary on the work you do.
Of course, you will have full editorial control over the content."

Chris bit his lip; she had found just the hook guaranteed
to snag him. For years he had been trying to interest the
media in covering Odin's work—a segment on a TV news-
magazine, a series of public-service announcements, anything. But he had a lot of competition; the world swarmed
with human interest stories. Struggling to maintain some
skepticism, he observed, "You intend to make your sister
into some kind of mascot for Odin?"

She frowned. "Spokesman. With this film she won't be thought of as a rock and roller anymore. She'll be accepted as a serious actress and, God knows why, actors are still considered more respectable than rockers. We talked about your need for corporate sponsors, as I recall. You've reached the limit of the funding you can get while Odin stays so low-profile. Corporations do some of their charitable giving out of genuine good spirit, it's true, but the rest is done for tax reasons and public relations. You've got to give them a public. Celebrities attract the public. I'm offering you the most tasteful, responsible mass-media event I can think of—if that isn't actually a contradiction in terms."

She left unsaid the sentence that naturally followed, but his own brain supplied it: if he turned down this proposal, he'd have proved himself unreasonable. He'd never find anything to please him. The trouble was, her plan *did* please him, in every respect but one. To stall, he said, "What do you plan to do with this documentary?"

"Show it on television—network, syndicated, cable, whatever. It'll be broadcast along with coverage of the premiere so the two events can reinforce each other."

Chris ground his teeth. "This is all a very grand fantasy, but..."

"It's not a fantasy at all. Look, I've got written commitments from Pioneer and Rosie and letters from two cable networks expressing interest in the idea. I wouldn't waste your time bringing you something half-baked."

She fell silent. The breeze from an opening door ruffled her thick, feather-light bangs, giving Chris a view of her watchful eyes, a view he didn't need. He *needed* to hide for a while and sort out his options, if he had any. Instead, he was thinking compulsively of Lorelei and what it would be like to work with her, to see her every day, to watch her small nose wrinkle as she frowned over a problem, to hear her husky voice ask him questions and to know that she would puzzle over his answers with all her terrifying earnestness.

Making an attempt to seem rational, he started asking questions. He asked the sharpest, toughest questions he knew, the kind that had made short work of the proposals he had rejected. But not this one. Lorelei had done her homework; she answered confidently and in great detail. They struggled through the meal, eating so little the waiter looked stricken when he took their plates away.

They walked back into town, still bashing her plan back and forth. Chris felt like a horse cornered in a box canyon. It was inconceivable that this girl, this *teenager* with her banana-colored disco outfit, had come up with the very plan Odin needed. But he knew that she was far more than *he* needed. He could not work with her. He would never be able to make it stop at work; she would disrupt his entire life. By some standards, Chris admitted, he might have a strange life, but it suited him. He had a job he believed in and the freedom to fly to his heart's content. If he rarely saw his house in Teeterbrouck, at least there was no one in it to feel slighted. Lorelei deserved a man who would be there for her, fuss over her, who would remember the names and hit records of the rock stars she knew, someone who could be charming at hip parties. On the rare occasions when he was grounded, Chris far preferred to wax his airplane than to go to parties.

As all these thoughts tumbled through his mind, Lorelei held the black folder under his nose. "Please, Chris. I guess you spoiled me. First you agreed to listen to Gil, then you took the time to explain why you were rejecting his proposal. Now I'm going to ask for one more favor. Look this over."

Chris took the folder. Oh, he would look at it all right. He would study it in excruciating detail, as if his life depended on it, hoping to find some fatal flaw. In some very important ways, his life *did* depend on it.

* * *

Rosie had left messages on Lorelei's answering machine: "Called to wish you luck today, but I guess you've already left;" "Figured you'd be home by now, but I guess it's a good sign that you're not. Call me with the news;" and finally, "Goodness, girl, I could go out and make another movie instead of hanging around here waiting for you! Call me!"

Lorelei reset the machine, then wrote thank-you notes to Macchio and to Owen Browne, *The Veldt*'s producer, who had put her in touch with him. Then she took her dripping umbrella and headed out onto the street. The oily gray clouds that had vanished from Teeterbrouck had moved south and settled stubbornly over Manhattan. Her usually cheerful neighborhood of Chelsea, with its potted geraniums and shining brass railings, looked dreary. Rosie's usually gray neighborhood of TriBeCa, a stretch of old industrial buildings slowly being turned into condominiums, was a dank wasteland. It suited Lorelei's mood perfectly.

Rosie opened the door of her loft and groaned. "I don't think I'm going to ask how it went. How many fingers of bourbon do you want?"

"How many fingers are left in the bottle?"

The loft was a bright playland of white cushions, gifts from fans and souvenirs her sister had carted back from Kenya. A stack of books on Africa, international health and fund-raising weighed down one coffee table. Rosie had thrown herself wholeheartedly into her new cause.

Lorelei barely saw a thing. She felt as if she had been wrapped in a shroud and buried. Rosie pushed her onto a couch and gave her a tumbler of whiskey. Then she perched next to the stack of books and watched Lorelei like a hawk in front of a rabbit hole. "Come on, girl—I'm about to fracture from the suspense. Did you find your Mr. Jansen?"

"I found him."

"Didn't he like the film?" Rosie's copper-colored eyes flashed.

"He liked it."

"Well, he must have liked the proposal, too. What's not to like? If you could sell it to a bunch of suspicious studio executives with beige personalities, someone who runs an offbeat operation like Odin should have fallen into your lap like a ripe plum."

Lorelei choked.

"No plum? Hmm..." Rosie devoted herself to a rare moment of quiet thought, gathering her enthusiasm for another surge. "Well, do you suppose it's the backwash from his experience with Gil that's making him such a hard sell?"

"I...don't think so. I think he's fair. He knew right away he couldn't use Gil's plan. He listened, but there was this awful sense of finality about it. Today was different. He *tried* not to like the plan. He grilled me like a prosecuting attorney." She raised fearful eyes to her sister. "Do you suppose the problem is me?"

"You? Why ever would he have a problem with you? You said yourself that you got along with him. He seemed to like you well enough to explain why he hated Gil's plan so you wouldn't think it was you."

"I don't know. Maybe this time it *is* me—maybe because I'm too young."

Rosie slapped the idea aside with a wave of her hand. "Half the execs at my record company are your age or younger. And didn't Jansen once say he thought you were capable? Is he a flatterer?"

"No..." Lorelei admitted in a weak voice. She sighed wearily. A sense of hopelessness had descended on her, and every movement seemed to take a huge amount of energy.

"Lorelei?" Rosie's voice brought her out of her fog. Her sister lanced her with a sharp stare. "Are you sick or something?"

"No, why?"

"Then have you been taken over by aliens? This is not the sister I used to hate because she was so well adjusted. You're not usually so hard on yourself when you run into problems. You do your best and you never take the bad stuff personally. You're so healthy-minded it makes me sick."

Lorelei gave a laugh that lacked conviction.

Rosie glared at her again. "*Is* there something personal in this deal?"

"Well, sure. You're my sister and your movie is very important."

"The hell with the movie! Is there something going on with this Chris Jansen guy?"

Lorelei jumped as if a bullet had struck the floor near her feet.

"Oh, honey, you're not stuck on him, are you? Is that why you want the job so bad?"

"It's a wonderful *job*. Why don't you think..." Rosie came over and wrapped a sisterly arm around her shoulders. The affectionate contact was enough to close Lorelei's throat with emotion. This is ridiculous, she told herself, I have no reason to get tragic about anything. Aloud, she said hoarsely, "Sorry, sis, must be low biorhythms or something."

"Biorhythms, right. Let me run through what you've told me about Chris, just to see if I've got it right. He's about thirty-seven, thirty-eight, a bachelor, gets in his plane and flies to Belize like some people go to the grocery, and before this whole Odin thing got started he was a cowboy in Chile?"

"Argentina."

"Same thing, honey—never-never land. Some men join the Foreign Legion..."

Lorelei's chin snapped up defensively. "And some join the Peace Corps. They're hardly the same type of men."

"Okay, okay! I didn't mean to accuse him of being a mercenary, just… Look, honey, it sounds like what you've got in Chris Jansen is your classic gypsy rover, very romantic but not very practical for a girl like you."

"What kind of a girl am I?"

"Serious. You make commitments, you carry them through. When you make friends, you'll die for them. There are some men who find that very scary."

Lorelei disentangled herself from her sister's arm and walked away. "But an employer ought to find it very desirable in someone he's thinking of hiring."

Rosie sighed in exasperation. "Oh, go ahead, *be* obtuse. But *he's* probably not. Does he know how you feel about him?"

"No!" Lorelei realized too late what she had just admitted. She hugged her arms defensively and declared through gritted teeth, "I can separate my personal feelings from my job, Rosie. I did it long enough with Gil."

"Yeah, but you *hated* Gil. It's not the same thing."

"I can deal with this, believe me. I'm going after the job because it's a good job. And if I get it I'll be too busy to have a personal life. You know how it is."

"I guess." Rosie didn't sound convinced.

But Lorelei told herself *she* was convinced. She had never let a private emotion cloud her reason or impair her ability before, and over the years with Gil the provocation had been great. Besides, she told herself, didn't familiarity breed contempt? So far she had only spent a few short hours with Chris—of course he still seemed perfect to her. But weeks and months of working together would undoubtedly reveal him to be a normal, flawed human being. Crushes petered out in the face of reality. And that was all it was, a crush.

None of this comforting philosophy relieved the tension that built up in Lorelei as she waited for Chris's answer. A week went by, a week in which she wandered the streets restlessly, watching movies that she couldn't remember later, trying on clothes that she didn't buy and having lunch with friends whom she left confused by her distracted behavior. She fretted and stewed—why was Chris taking so long? Was he taking the plan apart piece by piece and checking it with experts? Was he actually thinking about it at all? That was it, she decided—he had gone off to some remote country with one of the Odin jets and had forgotten the plan entirely. Having convinced herself that she would not hear his voice, she called the number of Odin's office in Teeterbrouck.

"Good morning, Odin Foundation." The voice was deep, but female and pleasantly raspy. Lorelei pictured a businesslike matron who chain-smoked. She explained to the voice who she was and asked if Chris was out of the country.

"No, hon, but I couldn't tell you where he *is* these days, or where his mind is, at least. He's been out at the Teeterbrouck airport fiddling with the airplane. You want the number? Maggie—she's the owner—will go out and bring him to the phone for you."

Lorelei took the number and called it, but rather than have this Maggie chase Chris down for her, she asked for instructions on how to get there herself. Then, without letting herself think about it too carefully, she got her sister's car out of its garage and started driving north out of the city. Not until she actually took the Teeterbrouck exit off the Palisades Parkway did she question her actions. Was it wise to corner Chris in his private lair? Wouldn't it ultimately be safer to sit tight and wait for his answer? If he said no and sat her down again to hear his explanation, she might not like what she heard at all.

Still debating, she followed her instructions through the back roads and found herself turning at a hand-painted sign that read Teeterbrouck Civil Airfield, M. West, Operator. In the blue sky that shone between the budding apple trees, a glider floated gracefully behind a tow plane. What would it be like to be so free? Lorelei wondered, alone on the air currents, without even engine noise to remind you that you were an earthling?

The casualness of the airport pleased her. The dirt parking lot held a motley assortment of cars and trucks, including a battered Alfa, and the main building, notwithstanding the bravely official sign over the porch, was a farmhouse. There were calico curtains at the windows and rocking chairs on the porch. Houston's Mission Control it was not.

Lorelei got out of the car and stood in the crisp cold, listening to the windsock snapping on the breeze. The pleasant smell of damp earth tinged the air, and the far-off whine of the tow plane only seemed to deepen the peace. She knew she had stumbled into the heart of Chris's private world, and she nearly got back into the car, reluctant to intrude. But a bony, middle-aged blond woman appeared on the porch holding something that looked like a thermos, and she called a cheery hello. Lorelei smiled and walked up the flagged path to the house.

"Good morning, I'm Lorelei Chant. I called earlier. I'm looking for Chris Jansen."

"Well, didn't *you* just drop in from heaven! I wanted to take this coffee out to him, but I'm running the Unicom all by myself today—the radio. He's in the second hangar over there, just past that orange airplane you can see in pieces in the tie-down area. Can't miss him." She thrust the thermos into Lorelei's hands. "Oh, I'm Maggie West. Glad to meet you. Have Chris bring you in later for pie." With an encouraging smile, she disappeared into the house, letting the storm door bang behind her.

Lorelei glanced ruefully at the big green thermos. Chris not only had an airplane here, he had a mom. Second hangar, huh? She squinted toward what Maggie had called the tie-down area and saw the orange hulk. Its wings lay beside it on cinder blocks. Other, whole airplanes stood around in the sparse grass like a snoozing herd of improbable beasts. Lorelei tripped over a metal loop embedded in a block of concrete—a hitching post? she wondered.

The sound of a radio greeted her from the huge splayed doors of the second hangar. Rock music... Chris listened to rock music? On the floor of the vast, echoing hangar she saw a couple of airplanes in pieces and one crisp white twin-engine that seemed in perfect condition. The radio sat on its wing. Chris's deep voice hummed along eccentrically.

Lorelei walked up to the plane and called inside, "I came to offer you a record contract, but now I'm not so sure."

Chris was almost upside-down, sprawled across the two front seats working with a mass of wires that hung from under the control panel. "Aw, and I was so looking forward to crossing over. Hang on a sec." He pulled himself out the opposite doorway, climbed out onto the wing and jumped down.

Lorelei tried to school herself to nonchalance, but her resolve fell apart when he walked around the nose of the plane to join her. The smile that creased his rough-shaven cheeks seemed tentative, not the usual easygoing Chris Jansen grin.

"You came a long way to bring me coffee."

"What? Oh." She thrust the thermos into his hands. "I met Maggie West when I drove in. This is from her. Actually, I'm turning the tables on you—I'm here to spy. I'm trying to observe the director of Odin in action."

"I see. Well, here you have the ultimate executive tool." He held up a pair of needle-nose pliers. "This is the best part of my job. I'd do it anyway...if I had my own airplane, that is."

"The rest of the job isn't fun?"

"Oh, all the other parts have their attractions, even reviewing event proposals." He gave her a candid look. "I expect you're wondering about that."

"It's crossed my mind. I'm not too good at waiting, I guess. Especially knowing how quickly you made a decision about *Gil's* plan." Chris's somber stare made her regret her bluntness. "This sounds like a confrontation, doesn't it? I'm sorry. Forget I even came up here...."

She started to turn away, but his hand reached out to catch the ends of her fingers and pull her back. "It's okay. I was going to tell you." He kept hold of her hand. "I'm about to give your proposal to my trustees for them to look over."

That was good, she told herself. Wasn't it? It must mean he had found no great flaw. Why then did she feel such a sense of foreboding? "But you have reservations about it?"

"Not about it. About us."

"What! Why? I thought we got along just fine. I thought..." That you liked me, she finished, not daring to say the words aloud.

But he heard them anyway, or saw them in her face. "I like you, Lorelei. I like you too much." His low, softly spoken answer struck her dumb. "You see, I don't know how to be fair to you. If I throw out your proposal it'll only be because I'm afraid of getting involved with you. If I accept it... you might find it a bit of a strain working with me."

Lorelei looked down at her shoes, sure she had been transported into someone else's body. Men like Chris Jansen did not say these things to women like her. The woman he should have been saying them to would have known how to reply. But the shoes were hers and the ineptness was hers as well. "That's very flattering, but you shouldn't tease me like that, Chris."

His eyes flared in surprise. "*Tease* you?"

"I'm not fishing for compliments or anything, but I'm hardly the kind of woman who... I mean I've never kept anyone awake nights...."

"Are you so sure? That's another one of our problems, you don't have any idea what you do to me." He took hold of her anxious hands again and slowly pulled her to him. She found herself resting with her arms barely keeping her from falling against his chest. His hands dropped to her waist and a shiver went through her.

"You make it sound so dramatic," she said desperately.

"Hasn't anyone ever thrown your life off center, Lorelei?" he murmured. He gave her no chance to answer; his hands at her waist pulled and toppled her the last few inches into his arms. His mouth came down on hers, gentle for a moment, as if testing her. Without thinking, she parted her lips, and Chris abandoned all caution. He reached one hand up to tangle strong fingers in her hair, then pulled her head back and opened her mouth to his demanding tongue. He was hardly gentle, but the fierceness of his kiss suited her.

He was so big and so vitally masculine he overwhelmed her. Her hands quivered upon his chest with the feel of his surging heart. It throbbed one hard beat for every two of hers. She moved her fingertips lightly over his velvet skin up to the pulse in his neck, conscious of the heat rising from him in the chill air. She stroked the silky hair behind his ear. Never before had she wanted a man to take control of her in this way, but the taste of Chris's tongue as he found every secret place in her mouth, the hard pressure of his lips, even the bite of his teeth barely began to answer the deep, primitive need she discovered inside her.

Then he firmly pushed her away. "You see what I mean? That wasn't fair—I thought I would be proving something.... But I was just trying to scare you off."

She blinked at him, bewildered. Rosie's warning came back to her. Chris was not the kind of man a woman got involved with unless she had as footloose an approach to life as he had. He was too wary of commitment, too in love with his freedom. A concrete reminder of what he truly valued loomed behind him: his gleaming white airplane. He had called it the Duchess, and it was probably the closest thing to a woman he would ever let into his life.

Chris launched himself away from the plane and took a few restless steps. Then he looked back in supplication. "I wanted *you* to make the decision for me, Lorelei. I hoped you'd decide to withdraw the proposal. You see? I'm not a reasonable man on this subject."

Lorelei heard her voice drift out, thin and weak. "I don't *expect* anything from you, Chris. I didn't submit the proposal in order to trade on . . . any feeling you might have for me. I just want to work for you, for the foundation. Can't we manage that?"

"I don't know, Lorelei."

"Your trustees could always reject the plan on their own," she suggested, trying to inject a weirdly optimistic note. She felt very shaky.

"Unfortunately, they'll do exactly what I *tell* them to do."

"Do I hear you showing off, Chris Jansen?" Maggie West's voice jolted them both out of their thoughts. She strolled into the hangar and looked at them curiously. "There's a phone call for you, Chris. And that pie is getting older by the minute. Are you coming up to the office?"

"Yeah, right now." Chris cast Lorelei a look, half appeal, half glower. "Give me a little longer to work this out, okay?"

She nodded numbly. She needed time to work it out herself.

Lorelei did not have nearly enough time, though she thought of little else. What had happened at the airport mystified and tormented her. Possibly all she could do was let it slowly recede in time and memory and then live with it as a mystery.

But two days later John Ward called. He asked her to meet him at Owen Browne's midtown office. She fought off a wave of nausea as she got ready, telling herself he probably just wanted to quiz her about the plan, perhaps to cover the medical aspects she had left sketchy. The fact that an Odin executive had asked to meet her in a Pioneer Films executive's office was significant, but Lorelei refused to dwell on it. She couldn't bear to think she might be facing the end of her wait, that in an hour she might know if she would ever see Chris again. Her feelings were so confused that she didn't know which outcome would make her happy. How had two people ever gotten themselves so tangled? she wondered. How had a job ever become so important?

Strictly speaking, she knew she could still back out of the whole thing. No contracts had been signed. She could always withdraw her proposal and say... say what? That a personal crisis prevented her from producing the premiere? A personal crisis—yeah, that was it.

Lorelei knew she'd do no such thing. She put on the soberest outfit she owned, a navy-blue dress with a demure lace collar, and took a taxi uptown.

After weeks of negotiating with Pioneer executives, their aggressively rustic offices on Sixth Avenue had become almost home to Lorelei. It no longer bothered her that the sleek computer terminals and word processors sat atop rough-hewn knotty-pine desks or that a large number of the employees wore cowboy boots. What surprised her was the collection of people that awaited her. Owen Browne and John Ward she had expected. But Rosie and the film director, Max Weiman? And Chris? Hadn't *he* grilled her enough? In the fake ruggedness of the decor, his genuine animal life force glowed like hot coals. He looked fabulous in his khaki-colored suit and shocking-lime-green shirt. He glared at her dress, as if annoyed that she had chosen one so out of character.

Lorelei broke their eye contact to greet the others, but found it hard to focus on anyone else. She hardly noticed the harsh look Rosie gave her.

"Ms. Chant, it's a pleasure to meet the author of this remarkable proposal!" Dr. Ward's bullhorn voice demanded her attention. He was a big, bluff man with the slight pomposity that sometimes afflicted doctors, but he was quite likable. She found that she could easily imagine him drinking with Chris in a noisy, disreputable Argentinian bar, knocking back tequilas amid a litter of half-chewed limes.

"Owen," Ward continued at full volume, "I just want to say before we start that I really appreciate the use of your office. People think it's strange that the foundation doesn't keep swank quarters in Manhattan, but they don't stop to think about the chunk it would take out of our budget. And who needs it? No one comes to us, anyway, we go to them. Or rather Chris does. Having him buzzing around in that little airplane is the greatest convenience we could ever have asked for."

Chris cleared his throat with some impatience and said, "Johnny..." He had backed away from the group and sat lightly upon the window ledge, staring down at his toes. In spite of herself, Lorelei smiled—Chris was wearing gold high-top sneakers.

"Oh, yeah, Chris reminds me that he's flying up to Montreal today to speak at a medical conference. I guess we should press on. Ms. Chant—"

"Lorelei."

"Lorelei...she was a siren in German mythology, wasn't she? Anyway, we're very excited about this plan of yours. We've been talking it over with Owen and Max and our lawyers, and everyone likes it. We're ready to go to contract if you are."

Lorelei failed to take this in. Rosie slapped her arm and cried, "Well, honey, don't just stand there wearing your sphinx face. Get out a pen!"

Then Lorelei realized what had happened—the trustees, anxious for their big event, had accepted a proposal over the reservations of their director. She darted a horrified glance toward Chris, expecting him to look as ominous as a thunderhead, but his expression was noncommittal. Then, unexpectedly, one corner of his mouth inched up. He was smiling at her reaction.

His smile broke the spell, she managed the proper exclamations of thanks, Browne's secretary walked in with a tray of champagne and glasses, and everyone toasted their new enterprise. Chris, clinking his glass against Lorelei's, murmured inexplicably, "Congratulations, you've saved my trustees from first-degree murder." She noticed, however, that he only took one small sip of the champagne. The irrational part of her was hurt; the rational part reminded her that he had to fly that day. When he abruptly excused himself and strode out of the office, she was torn between relief and despair.

The champagne finally ran out, and Dr. Ward walked her to the elevator. Lorelei felt that she was, in some sense, walking with Chris's other half—the half that actually looked forward to working with her. Dr. Ward was full of enthusiasm and curiosity. She sighed.

"That's a mighty depressing sound, miss. You're not happy with the arrangements?"

"It's not that.... I'd just rather not be forcing myself down Chris's throat."

"Forcing yourself down...I heard him admit that you had saved us from murder. It's true! These past months we've been ready to stake him to an anthill. My God, he rejected seven proposals! Eight! Two evenings ago, when he called me and said he had finally found one that would work, I thought it must be a wrong number."

Two evenings ago? she thought. That would have been the night of their disaster at the airport. He had decided to accept her plan then?

Ward took brusque but affectionate hold of her shoulder. "In all the years I've known Christian Jansen, I've learned to trust his word and ignore his moods. He doesn't have very many moods, actually. If he's a little distracted right now, I'm inclined to indulge him. Don't you worry, Lorelei, he'll come out of it and you'll see the Chris we all know and love."

She managed to smile, but as soon as she got on the elevator by herself her smile collapsed. She stopped in the lobby to pick up the latest edition of Billboard and flipped through it, hoping to distract herself. The next issue would carry the notice of her coup upstairs in the Pioneer offices: "Owen Browne has announced that Lorelei Chant Productions will promote the upcoming feature film *The Veldt* from Pioneer Films, the premiere to benefit the Odin Foundation" or something like that. A tiny flash of pleasure shot through her as she imagined Gil's face when he saw the copy.

"So you *do* remember how to smile." Her sister's voice drawled in her ear.

"It's just gas. Isn't that what they say about babies?"

Rosie raked her with a mercilessly sharp look. "Honey, we're not talking babies. Something tells me you've got a great big grown-up problem."

Lorelei swatted her sister with the magazine. "This place is swarming with Pioneer employees. Can we discuss it outside?" She led her sister out onto the street and turned south, automatically heading for home. After she had put several blocks between herself and Pioneer, she ventured a timid question. "Was the atmosphere back there as bad as I thought it was?"

"Honey, there was stuff flying between you and the lovely Mr. Jansen that could have knocked out a tank." She gave Lorelei a sharp pinch and hissed, "Why didn't you *tell* me he was so gorgeous? I might have given you different advice."

"Oh, yeah? Like what?"

"Well, I'm not exactly sure . . . either to bury yourself in a fallout shelter until he left town or to throw yourself at him shamelessly and enjoy him for as long as you can."

"What do you think about *working* for him?"

"Don't expect too much of yourself—you're only human."

"Born to make mistakes."

"Yeah. So now that you've got yourself into this, what are you going to do?"

"I'm going to work!" Lorelei felt her resolve coming back.

"And God help anyone who gets in your way, including Chris Jansen?"

"Including him."

"Well..." Rosie struggled. "Well..."

"Well what?"

"Well—what are you going to do first?"

Lorelei's brain began to do what it did best, organize. She had to pull together a film crew, brief them on Odin, make sure they had valid passports. She had to find out from Dr. Ward when the next mission left and if her crew could join it. She had to start making presentations to potential corporate sponsors.

At the foot of Lorelei's steps, Rosie bade her goodbye and hailed a cab. Preoccupied with planning, Lorelei unlocked the door of her brownstone and stepped into the foyer. The smell of curry poured up from the apartment below, filling the stairwell from the bottom to the top floor. Lorelei climbed through it, slowly realizing that she was hungry. When she reached her own landing, she stared in amazement. The curry smell had masked that of what stood by her door, a huge bouquet of white and yellow flowers: snapdragons, hollyhocks, primroses and irises. She dug a card out from under the cascading lemon-yellow bow. It read:

If you've got guts enough to put up with me, you've already licked this job. *Pax*, Chris.

Lorelei sat down on the top step with a thump. *Pax?* Would there ever be any peace in her life while there was Chris?

Chapter Four

The first few days of being Odin's event producer passed in a familiar, comfortable fever. Lorelei put her office in order. She shoved the bed against the wall of her studio apartment and bought a lot of cardboard file cabinets. She hired a film crew and introduced herself over the telephone to Elsie Carmichael, Chris's craggy-voiced secretary. Elsie had been with Odin for six years, she told Lorelei, ever since Chris had found that while he traveled work piled up to towering heights. She knew the organization inside and out and promised Lorelei a rush shipment of old files and promotional material to get her started.

Lorelei felt cowardly for dealing with Chris's secretary rather than with him. She had even sent her filmmakers up to Teeterbrouck alone for a preliminary story conference. She told herself she had too much to do in Manhattan; once things got underway, there would be plenty of time to see him. By then it would even be easier—she would have stacks of legitimate business concerns to take up with him. That was what she told herself, anyway.

Howard and Deana, the filmmakers, threw themselves into the project as wholeheartedly as Rosie had. It seemed to Lorelei that one day they were listening to her background spiel about missions to Brunei and East Timor and the Marshall Islands and the next day they were leaving messages on her machine about the World Health Organization and dengue fever. In no time at all they told her they were ready to go on the next Odin mission. Lorelei checked her calendar. She had been on the project for barely two weeks. May had arrived, and a few brave city flowers were sparkling against the concrete and brick.

"You're all ready to go?" she asked Howard again, just to make sure.

"Yeah, can you round up your rock-star sister and put her on the plane with us?" he asked briskly. "We want to get footage of her in a real mission setting—showing the medical team at work, touring the villages, all that stuff, you know?"

"She's in L.A. singing on a friend's new album. She's not due back until the eleventh."

Howard made an exasperated sound. "She'll miss the start of the mission by two days. Can't you call her back early?"

"Hardly. What's so urgent about *this* mission? It's the ophthalmology plane, right? Elsie tells me the other plane is flying a plastic-surgery run to Ecuador in three weeks. Ecuador is picturesque; can't you start the documentary there?"

"Ecuador is also wet and mountainous, and that would increase our technical problems about nine zillion times. Besides, this island—St. Simon—where the eye plane is going, is just like a miniature Jamaica or Haiti. In fact, it's near Haiti. It'll all look amazingly familiar to the audience. When they think about the vacations they've spent drinking piña coladas in the sun and buying straw hats, they'll be horrified that they were only a mile away from the kind of poverty and health problems we're going to show them. Chris is very adamant about making that kind of point in the documentary."

"Hmm. I see." Chris's ideas figured prominently in Howard and Deana's calculations; Lorelei's "independent filmmakers" had become his devout disciples.

"And besides, Lorelei, the weather's great there—dry, sunny, not too hot. Hurricane season doesn't start for another month."

"Look, *I'm* convinced, but it's more likely that you can get Odin to push back *its* schedule than get Rosie out of L.A."

Howard grumbled and made some vague remarks about talking to Chris. After he had hung up, Lorelei suffered a moment of panic; what if he *did* suggest a change in the mission schedule? God forbid! Lorelei had promised that her project would interfere as little as possible with the work of the foundation. Suggesting that nine doctors, five nurses, five technicians and three flight-crew members reschedule their mission counted as definite interference. Lorelei calmed herself by remembering that, as gung ho as Howard might be, he wasn't an idiot.

The next day Chris called. Lorelei went rigid—maybe Howard *was* an idiot.

"I understand we've got a scheduling conflict," he observed. His voice was perfectly calm and pleasant.

"Er...yes, Rosie's hung up in California until the end of next week." She wondered if he could hear the sudden thunder of her heart. The sound of his voice was adrenaline to her; it could have been bottled and sold as a stimulant. "I suggested we do the filming on your Ecuador trip, but..."

"Oh, no need for that," he drawled easily. "Howard and Deana can fly down to St. Simon with the jet and get started. Then, when your sister gets back to New York, I'll fly the two of you down in the Duchess."

The two of them? Lorelei was speechless. The vision of herself in the tiny cockpit elbow to elbow with Chris for thousands of miles emptied her of all sense.

"What's the matter, project coordinator? You afraid to fly with me?" He had read her mind. "I've got a valid twin-engine commercial license with an instrument rating, thirty-five hundred hours in that particular airplane, and I haven't crashed yet."

She forced herself to let out her strangled breath. "I'm sure you're a very worthy descendant of Charles Lindbergh, but I just... There's a lot of work to do up here...."

"A sickly excuse if I ever heard one. You, of all people, ought to have firsthand experience of an Odin mission. Think of how convincing you'll be when you tell potential sponsors how it feels to watch as our surgeons take the bandages off a cataract patient and to see *her* see again for the first time in fifteen years."

"Well, uh... that would be useful," she mumbled.

"Is that a yes?"

"I guess so...."

Rosie finished her singing in L.A. Chris spent a couple of days in Houston recruiting volunteers from a nursing school. In New York, Lorelei saw the final edit of *The Veldt*, the version that would be entered in the Madrid Film Festival. Then each of the three made a separate trip to Opa Locka, Florida, to meet for the last leg of the journey.

"Chris—recruiting student nurses?" Rosie chuckled. She and Lorelei were walking across the breezy blacktop behind the airport's small terminal building. She wore huge dark glasses to disguise the fact that she was still on West Coast time. "Poor little nurses, they wouldn't have stood a chance. Must have been like shooting fish in a barrel."

Her verdict was reinforced by their first sight of Chris's bronzed figure in the Duchess. He stuck his head out of the cockpit and waved. The skintight white tank top made it

clear why everything he wore looked so classy—he had a
very classy body. His stomach looked tight and as flat as the
runway, his arms were hard and powerful beneath their
slight sunburn, and his shoulders were broad. Lorelei
wanted to drink in the sight of him in the honey-gold sunlight. Instead, she dropped her gaze to the tarmac.

"Good morning, ladies. Which one of you is going to be
my copilot on this trip?" As he asked, he grabbed their bags
and ducked into the back of the airplane to stow them.

"Lorelei is," Rosie volunteered, causing her sister a flash
of horror. "I'm an old hand at this aviation business. Bored
by the wonders, you know? But she's virgin territory."

Lorelei hissed, "I thought you were my *friend*."

"No—*sister*. There's an important difference."

"Remind me to ask you what it is."

Rosie gave her an enigmatic smile. Chris reappeared in the
doorway and helped her into the plane. Before Lorelei had
prepared herself, he came back for her. Taking a deep
breath, she extended her hand. He pulled her up onto the
wing as if she had no weight, and steadied her with a hand
on her waist. She stared into his unfathomable blue eyes and
remembered the last time he had touched her so. As if he
remembered it, too, he dropped his hand. Then he ducked
inside the Duchess. Lorelei followed slowly.

Cramped didn't half describe the cabin of the little plane.
The seats were narrow and squashed together. When Lorelei had slid into one, she found herself faced with a verita-
ble wall of controls eighteen inches in front of her nose.
How long was the flight? she wondered. Three hours? Four?
Three or four hours with Chris's red-gold body an inch from
hers? Impossible. A normal person she could ignore, but he
had a shimmering presence, a hot, edgy masculinity that
took command of the space and everything in it—including her. She pretended to study the controls intently.

"If you're so interested, you can read off the checklists to me." He handed her a spiral-bound book of plastic-coated pages.

She scanned the items rather than have to look at him. "'Cyl head temp in green arc'? I don't know what this means."

"Then let's hope I do."

He seemed determined to establish a light tone, and Lorelei was glad to cooperate. Following his lead, she strapped herself down and muffled her ears under a radio headset. This seemed to amuse him, but he clicked a couple of switches and she heard his voice over the headphones. "Okay, start reading."

Rosie leaned forward to tap Chris on the shoulder. Lorelei marveled that her sister could touch him so easily when she was sure her own finger would have burst into flame. "We're ready to go? Just like that?"

Chris looked theatrically aggrieved. "What 'just like that'? I've been up for three hours preflighting the airplane, checking on the weather and filing a flight plan. Come on, copilot, read."

Lorelei obeyed promptly. "Flight controls free."

"Check."

"Flaps up."

"Check."

And so they continued, Lorelei bluffing her way through the jargon. The checklist seemed to set a businesslike buffer between them—or it did until she read the item that said "Doors locked." Chris reached across her lap to lock *her* door, his golden arm lightly brushing her breasts. Air would no longer enter her lungs. Her next couple of commands were weak.

When she got to the item "Clear props," Chris cranked open a window vent and, although no one stood anywhere near the plane, roared out, "Clear!" The engines thundered to life and the propellors became spinning blurs. Chris radioed the tower for takeoff clearance and runway instructions. Over the headset, Lorelei heard a voice reply in a fierce burst of static. Chris answered, "Roger, three-eight-seven," and taxied to the top of the runway. For a few seconds he revved the Duchess's engines, then sent the machine rumbling down the centerline. Lorelei gripped the checklists, straining as hard as the engines, as if she could lift the plane with her own effort. A short distance down the runway, the nose came up and the heavy vibrations fell away; the plane was airborne, climbing. Lorelei felt exhilarated and wonderstruck.

Chris flew them along the hazy silver skyline of Florida's Gold Coast—Palm Beach, Fort Lauderdale, Miami Beach. Then he peeled away from the mainland and struck out for the long splatter of fragile green islands that made up the Bahamas. Sunlight spangled the water, and the sky was a harsh, deep sapphire, the utterly cloudless blue Chris called "severe clear."

Lorelei never read a page of the book she'd brought. The vivid feeling of being aloft—so different than the bland ride one got in a big jet—kept her mesmerized. She could feel every air current that washed over the plane, causing it to buck or tip or suddenly drop. She wondered if birds felt this way. The noise of the engines made it impossible to talk when she took off the headphones and so she was able to simply bask in Chris's reassuring presence, sharing with him the complete, if noisy, peace.

Periodically he pointed out other aircraft in the skies and ships and schools of dolphins below, and as they reached the northern curve of the Caribbean archipelago he identified the islands for her: Little Inagua and Great Inagua, Ambergris Cay, Turks Island. They were swaths of lush green hills fringed by white beaches and sandbars that turned the shallow waters around them into peacock tails of iridescence.

Finally he pointed ahead to a dark buckle on the horizon and announced that it was St. Simon. Lorelei reached around to wake her sister. Chris chatted on the radio, and this time Lorelei deciphered some of the words. She decided it must be like learning to understand what rock stars mumbled into the microphone at a concert—you had to get some practice.

Chris flew lower and lower until the island expanded across their entire field of vision. Lush hilly forests alternated with patchworks of pale green fields and cleared red earth. Here and there Lorelei saw small white shapes that proved to be houses and tiny moving motes that were cars.

As Chris flew over one last sinuous ridge, Lorelei saw the Odin jet. It sat like a white cross near the end of a long clearing that had been gouged straight through the forest— the runway. Lorelei wondered at the nerves of the Odin pilot who'd had to land on such a thing. Hills huddled close on either side, the ocean sparkled at one end and the jungle loomed at the other.

"This isn't the island's only airport, is it?" she shouted.

"No, that's about an hour's drive from here in Bolestown. But this island was an Allied flight-training base during the Second World War. The authorities very wisely kept up the runway, more or less. The town's called Simonville. What do you think of it?"

Lorelei hedged. "It's . . . colorful." Chris grinned. Even at this altitude, the village that sprawled down the side of the nearest hill looked like a tumbled set of children's blocks. The houses peeked out from clumps of flowering bushes, following no street plan at all, and as Chris banked in closer Lorelei saw that they were little more than shacks, brightly painted but ramshackle. A couple of Quonset huts sat by the airfield.

"Here goes," Chris announced. "Watch out for livestock on the runway."

The warning shook Lorelei, and she spent the whole landing tensely on the lookout for charging herds of cattle. None appeared, and Chris's landing was as smooth as silk, but the sudden transition from airborne to landbound creature left her numb. It took her a minute to realize that the white figures waving from between the two Quonset huts were Howard and Deana and several Odin people in lab coats.

"Your camera team is really on top of things," Chris remarked, taxiing toward them. "They're already filming us."

"Oh, my God!" They heard Rosie scrambling through her pocketbook. "I must look like I flew here without an airplane."

Lorelei tried to ignore the cameras as she jumped to the ground. She intended to make Deana cut every second of her own presence from the video. It was Rosie who mattered, and Rosie, despite her fuss about the way she looked, completely took over the spotlight as soon as she stepped onto the wing. Lorelei stood to one side watching, disliking life on the ground more with each passing second. It was ninety-five degrees in the humid, airless valley, sand flies stung her ankles and the sunshine pierced her sunglasses like darts.

Chris joined her on the sidelines, looking as bright and golden as a splinter off the sun itself. He had brought their bags. The white lab-coated figures and two more in grease-stained T-shirts swarmed to greet him and introduce themselves to Lorelei.

"Hold on! Hold on!" Chris ordered good-naturedly. "The lady's still up in the clouds. Let me get her settled before you all descend on her." He looked over the heads of his colleagues to check on Rosie. "Our star looks busy. I'll come back for her later. Come on, Ms. Producer, I've got you booked at the St. Simon Hotel. Don't expect too much."

"Where are all the mission people staying?" she asked.

"The St. Simon. But for the team it's less a matter of *staying* than of dropping in every few days for a shower."

She struggled to follow him as his long strides carried him quickly over the hummocky ground. Makeshift tents and vehicles sprawled in a messy caravan farther down the runway. "What's all that?"

"Our patients. They start coming long before the jet gets here and they hang around until it leaves, hoping we'll fit them into the surgery schedule. No matter how packed we get, slots always open up—someone will run a fever, and we'll have to cancel their surgery or a surgeon will decide he can manage one more procedure that day. Still, there's too many people who go away disappointed. You can't be soft-hearted or this kind of work would depress you."

You *have* to be softhearted, Lorelei corrected silently, or you wouldn't *do* this kind of work.

Chris led her up a street of hand-packed dirt. It wound in and out among pastel-painted houses and tiny shacks. Children in randomly sized clothing stopped their play to stare and sometimes wave shyly. Chris waved back. Their walk ended in front of a single-story building, whitewashed and covered in poinciana.

"How do you know your way around here so well, Chris?"

"I came down to make the arrangements—talking to the ministry of health, measuring the runway, all that stuff. I'm always the advance scout." He swung open the screen door and held it for her. As hotels went, the St. Simon was a pretty casual affair. The bar doubled as the registration desk, the bartender as the concierge. He took room keys off a hook next to a bottle of pineapple rum and gave them to Chris. Chris wordlessly gave them to Lorelei and led the way back into the brilliant sunshine.

The rooms were cabanas reached by walkways that had been tunnelled through a thicket of sea grape and bougain-villea. Lizards scuttled out from under Lorelei's feet, but after the first scare she didn't flinch. When they reached her cabana, Chris walked in quite naturally to deposit her suitcase. She followed, wondering if he would offer to unpack for her as well. A strange sight interrupted the thought. "Chris, is that what I think it is over the bed?"

"Yep, mosquito netting. Welcome to paradise. Make sure you shake out your sheets before you go to bed, and your clothes and shoes, too."

"What am I supposed to be shaking out?" she asked uneasily.

His smile flashed. "Scorpions and spiders. I'll be back with your sister."

Lorelei was left alone looking at the threadbare chenille bedspread, the straw mats on the floor and the bits of furniture, which looked as if they had been bought at a garage sale. The fan in the ceiling slowly churned the torrid air, but lousy conditions had never fazed her. Life with Gil had taken her to the worst backstage hellholes and laminated cardboard motels. If Chris's doctors could operate with horseflies buzzing around their heads and sweat staining their scrubs dark green, she could remember to shake out her shoes.

She had just dressed after a quick shower when Rosie appeared at her doorstep and hammered on the screen. "Come on, princess. Enough with this beauty routine of yours, we've got work to do." Rosie looked annoyingly fresh; being the center of attention had always brought out the best in her. "Did you pack any sunscreen, sis? Deana tells me I've got to stay the same color throughout the documentary, and I swear you could fry an egg on the end of my nose."

Lorelei let her in and shared the sunscreen. "Whew, now we both smell like a bag of moth balls."

"Yeah, well, I intend to finish the taping and then spread myself all over that gorgeous beach. I'm going to get as wicked a tan as your lover boy."

"Rosie!" Lorelei gasped in horror.

Rosie fell silent, honestly perplexed.

"Don't call him that!"

"What? You mean...oh, Lord. You're never going to be able to handle this if you can't joke about it."

"I *can* handle it, but that doesn't mean you need to...go on about it."

Rosie sniffed, unconvinced, and flounced out of the cabana.

Chris met them near the jet. He grinned at Lorelei. "This time *I* get to ask. How are you with blood?"

He remembered! She flushed with pleasure. "Bleeding it or drinking it?"

Rosie frowned at the two of them.

"Just looking at it."

"You've seen how it is backstage at a concert. Both of us are rock veterans."

"Then I'll give you the *whole* tour."

With that provocative promise, he led them through the Quonsets that had been appropriated for mission use. They saw the dilapidated lounge where the staff retreated for bad coffee—it looked no worse than any backstage dressing room. Then he showed them the triage room where prospective patients were screened. It was filled by people with wounds and complaints of all types, many having nothing to do with ophthalmology. Lorelei wondered if triage was the part Chris left out when he gave tours to the squeamish.

But no, she discovered that he had meant the jet itself. It was a classroom for surgery. When he led them into what had once been the first-class cabin, she and Rosie joined a group of St. Simonian doctors. On video monitors they watched a cornea transplant being performed in the operating theater behind them. Lorelei could well believe that this was where a lot of people left the tour. Rosie hid behind a blind corner, but Lorelei watched the procedure in fascination. She wished she had a headset so she could hear

the surgeon's explanations as he cut and closed incisions
with a tiny laser. It seemed incredible that such a miracle of
science could exist side by side with tar-paper shacks.

Chris finally had to drag her away. Outside, he remarked, "You know, there's still time for you to get into
med school."

"I can't see that there's much difference in the quality of
life." She thought of the nurse she had seen passed out on
the musty couch in the lounge, of the doctor examining a
crying child while another screamed in his ear. "High stress,
little sleep, no food. At least backstage at a concert there's
always food around—it's part of a band's contract."

"That's right, Chris Jansen!" Rosie chimed in. "Even
Gilman *fed* us. Is there a fast food burger place on this
island?"

Chris exchanged glances with Lorelei. "These tempera-
mental stars! I thought you rock people liked to stay
skinny."

"Neither my sister nor I is *in* rock anymore," Lorelei replied meaningfully. Skinny? She dwelled on his comment
even as he led them back into town. She was *not* skinny. She
didn't see how she could be any fatter and look right in the
clothes she owned—the slim-legged jeans, the short skirts,
the slinky dresses bought for important parties. Tiny fingers of doubt began to wiggle in her mind. Was her style
perhaps just a bit too... adolescent?

She fretted sporadically as they ate dinner on the tree-
screened patio of the St. Simon. Every time Chris's speculative eyes flickered over her she wondered what he saw. She
wanted to look competent and trustworthy to his co-
workers; she didn't want them to think Odin's financial future had been put in the hands of a raw kid, although she
was younger than nearly everyone else on the mission. But
on the other hand she didn't want to look *dull*. She didn't
want Chris's gaze to land on her and slide right off again,
bored. It was an impossible problem, and she told herself

sternly that she shouldn't even be worrying about what Chris thought of her as a woman. She was here as a producer. She pulled herself together. "Howard and Deana said earlier that they have a lot of tape on the activity here. Tomorrow they want to start working on the speaking parts."

Rosie got a glow of anticipation in her eyes.

"Fine with me," Chris agreed. "What are *you* going to do?"

"Get in the way. What else does a producer do?"

"Maybe Chris can keep you busy," Rosie suggested.

Lorelei barely choked back her gasp of dismay, but her sister had spoken in a tone of blandest innocence. What an actress she was! Lorelei thought. "I rather imagine Chris has plenty to do without having to entertain me."

Chris's amiable answer put her at ease once again. "You're more than welcome to help Bud and me work on the airplanes. I'll bet you're handy with a lug wrench."

"Only to hit muggers with. No, I think I'll roam around—absorb the atmosphere and make a pest of myself. I *do* want to have lots of firsthand stories for when I try to sell this project to sponsors." Chris nodded cheerfully. Lorelei sat back and ate the rest of the meal trying not to worry about her weight.

She spent the next day doing exactly as she'd planned. She haunted the triage room, watched the doctors and nurses interview hopeful patients and listened to alternately hair-raising and funny stories about previous missions. She talked to the St. Simonians who had set up makeshift camps. They begged her to intercede on behalf of the relatives they had brought from miles away—old people with cataracts, children with crossed eyes and blurry vision. She felt like a criminal every time she had to explain that she had no influence with the doctors.

A day of it was more than she could bear. That evening, not even the camaraderie at dinner could dispel her sense of frustration and her low mood. No one else seemed so afflicted. Rosie, Howard and Deana discussed the film script, the day's taping, camera angles and lighting. The medical staff exchanged their own technical talk. Lorelei chewed on her salad and sank deeper into her thoughts. Afterward she excused herself from coffee and went out for a walk along the deserted beach.

She wandered up and down a couple of times, watching the last rays of sunlight gild the tops of the waves. The sound of a voice beside her took her by surprise.

"I think my plan backfired."

She swung around to see that Chris had fallen into step beside her. The sun caught the strong planes of his face and gave them a new, ruddier color. No, she decided, the color came from sunburn. "What do you mean your plan backfired? What plan?"

"I wanted to show you the work we do. I know it's a long haul for you between now and the premiere, and there'll be plenty of rough spots. I wanted you to be able to look back on this trip and know exactly what you were working so hard for. But instead you're depressed."

"Don't you ever get depressed? Or discouraged? There are so many people camped out back there, hoping to see your doctors. And St. Simon is only one little island. You could run a hundred of these airplanes year round and hardly make a dent in the problem."

"I know," he sighed. "But depression is just not something we can afford to indulge in. Your problem is you haven't been truly busy—when you're working from the second you wake up to the second you collapse on a camp bed, you have no time to think about the size of the overall problem. And you *do* see the successes. You patch up some little girl who's nearly lost an eye and you know she's going to grow up fully sighted and pretty. That's not a little achievement. Things like that keep you going."

"Yeah, I guess…" She determinedly shook off her mood; strolling on a tropical beach with Chris was no occasion for gloom. "But *you* won't be able to keep going much longer if you don't take better care of yourself."

"Huh?"

"Look at that sunburn!" A flare of red crossed his cheeks and the long, straight bridge of his nose; it cut off sharply under his eyes where his sunglasses had sat. She blessed the impulse that had made her bring a hat and a tube of sunscreen. If Chris's well-tanned skin could burn in St. Simon, her own would have been charred off.

"Oh, it's not so bad."

"No?" She reached over and laid the edge of her fingernail against the skin of his shoulder. An unnatural heat poured from him. She had no intention of scratching him, but he flinched reflexively. "Uh-huh. Come on, Mr. Stoic. I've got something you can put on that burn."

He raised his eyebrows but obediently followed her back to the cabanas. Only when she had unlocked her own door and strode into her dim little room did she glance back and find him hanging uncertainly in the doorway. How strange, she thought, to see such a big man—a skilled pilot, the founder and head of the Odin Foundation—stricken with uncertainty. "Well come on. The bugs are getting in."

He let the screen door shut behind him. His eyes watched her, suddenly wary, and she felt herself lose all her blithe confidence. She nervously turned her attention to her suitcase and spent a few moments finding the tube of lotion. When she pulled it out and turned, she saw that he had come very close. She held out the tube, but he didn't take it. "You can put it on just as a moisturizer," she babbled. "But it's got some kind of medicine in it that will numb your skin a little." Why didn't he take it? she wondered. His expression was odd, a bit speculative, a bit … afraid? Lorelei faltered. She could resist his humor, his rugged self-confidence, but this uncertainty, this hint of vulnerability snatched at her

heart. "Will you be able to reach your back?" she asked
feebly.

It took him a long time to answer. "I don't think so."

She adopted what she hoped was a professionally brisk
manner. "Then I'll do it. Take off your shirt."

Chris's eyes narrowed, and he seemed to brace himself.

"Come on," she prompted. "Think of me as your
doctor."

Giving her a smoldering look that she *knew* he wouldn't
have given a doctor, Chris took the edge of his tank top and
pulled it over his head in one fluid movement. The flow of
his muscles beneath the smooth skin mesmerized her until
she heard his low groan. The poor man *was* badly burned,
she reminded herself. She had no business thinking about
the possibilities of... of anything.

"Sit down." She pointed to the bedspread, all business.
"I can't believe you're surrounded by doctors and they let
this happen to you. They all need *their* eyes examined. You
may *think* you're tan enough to be immune to the sun, but
blondes should treat it like *poison*, do you hear me?" He
groaned again.

Her composure lasted until she actually put her lotion-
smeared hands against his warm shoulders. Simply touching a man should not have been so intoxicating, she thought
in agony. Kissing him, making love with him, yes...but just
touching? Chris's flesh felt like life itself to Lorelei: warm—
too warm—tender, soft as breath yet flowing with power
underneath. Every stroke her hands made over his broad,
sloped shoulders was a wonder and a trial. The waves of
honey-colored hair that curled over his neck begged to be
pulled, the graceful curve of his back to be traced with
spellbound fingers. She was afraid that at any moment she
might lean down involuntarily and softly bite him. He gave

a low sigh of relief as the lotion doused the flame in his skin. Lorelei wished it would cool her down as well.

Her job as "doctor" ended with his back, but when she started to draw away he turned silently, caught her hand and pulled it slowly across his chest. Robbed of will, Lorelei let him. Her fingers felt the smooth, hard muscles, the edges of his wing-shaped collarbones, the deep thrum of his heart beneath his ribs. His eyes, so close to hers, were the black and silver blue of the sky at the edge of space. She reached up to his cheeks and stroked the lines of his nose and jaw, all pretense of treating his sunburn gone. The dark lashes flickered as his eyes searched hers, and his perfect, seductive mouth almost seemed to tremble.

When she felt his big hands circle her waist and pull her across his lap, her dreamlike state vanished. One strong arm cradled her like a baby as she tumbled backward, off balance; the other sent gentle fingers over her cheek and her ear and then into her damp hair. The soft brush of his breath felt almost as warm as she imagined his lips would if he would only kiss her. But he did not. Suddenly he took hold of her wrists and forced her arms down, a fierce tension vibrating through him. He glared into her eyes. "This is going to keep happening to us, Lorelei."

Her cheeks flamed, and she struggled to her feet. Good God, it *had* happened again! She had melted into his arms as if...as if she belonged there. She hadn't thought once of her own proud declarations that she could handle her feelings, that she wouldn't jeopardize her job. She swallowed hard. "No, it won't." He looked less than convinced. She searched for words to mollify him. "Blame it on the location—tropical island and all. No one acts normal in a place like this."

He got to his feet. "How can you tell what should be normal between us, Lorelei?" Taking his shirt, he quietly walked out.

The screen door closed between them like a fortress gate; Lorelei stared at it, her mouth half-open. What *was* normal between them? Was there any safe answer?

Chapter Five

As soon as Lorelei's taxi brought her within sight of the hard, gray New York skyline, she found it incredible that the events on St. Simon had ever happened. What a different world it was there. In New York she could keep her perspective. The very shape of its streets—arrow-straight with blocks as regular as a checkerboard—reminded her that she was a *businesswoman*. Only in the fuzzy borderland of a place like Teeterbrouck or the out-and-out fantasy world of St. Simon could she have found herself in the arms of her boss. There would be no further confusion, she told herself. Chris didn't want to get involved with a woman who could threaten his freedom? Well, she vowed, there would be no woman available, just a professional producer who would let nothing get between her and her job.

With this resolve made, Lorelei decided the time had come to meet the redoubtable Elsie Carmichael and to see the Teeterbrouck office. She told herself the fact that Chris was safely in St. Simon for another week had nothing to do with her timing. Over the telephone, Elsie gave her driving instructions that sounded even wilder than the ones to the airfield, a jumble of railroad crossings and turns at barns and forks in the road.

But, as Lorelei expected, Elsie's instructions worked perfectly. After driving through apple orchards and hills covered with bracken-tangled woods, Lorelei reached a snaking driveway lined by very old, very tall lilac bushes. The driveway jogged around and over granite outcroppings until it poured out into a clearing in the woods—a yard. A two-story house of white clapboard crowned a slight rise in the middle of the lawn. Its several wings and porches were braced by rose trellises and rambled as if the house had been spread out like a picnic blanket rather than built. A sensible car sat by the back door. It looked like the sort of car Elsie Carmichael might drive, so Lorelei parked next to it and got out.

A woman emerged from the doorway. She was as sensible-looking as the car, neat, thin and old enough to get away with calling Chris "that boy." She took one look at the silver Mercedes and said bluntly, "The producer business must be good. How much are we paying you?"

"Oh, this is my sister's car—suitable to her status as a movie star, she says. Since I'm promoting her movie, I'm going to borrow her wheels when I come up here."

"You're going to be putting a lot of miles on that car, honey."

"No, I'm going to do most of the work out of my office in Manhattan."

Elsie trained cool brown eyes upon her and said, "Dumbest plan I ever heard. Everything you need is up here, girl—phones, files, space, *me*. I can't imagine what Chris has on his mind if he thinks you can be running back and forth like a messenger. Oh, well, come see the office."

Lorelei was impressed. A sun porch and the big room beyond had been transformed into a workplace of unimpeachable order and clarity, yet the homey look had been preserved. The furniture was standard American den, but the photocopier and the small computer were Madison Avenue.

"This must be a very pleasant place to work," Lorelei commented.

"I'd be a fool to complain. Now that the warm weather's settled in I crank open the windows on the sun porch and it's just heavenly. Town isn't far away if I want to run out for a bite, but mostly I raid Chris's refrigerator. Speaking of which, you want some coffee and a sandwich before you look through the photo files?"

Lorelei opened her mouth to decline, but Elsie hadn't waited. She scurried after the brisk secretary and stopped dead in the middle of the next room. Elsie peered at her curiously.

"*Now* I believe Chris lives here," Lorelei laughed. The open-beamed, rustic room had almost no furniture—just a chair with a reading light, a couple of stereo speakers and a couch that sat in front of a clean-swept fieldstone fireplace. But it was *full* of airplanes: toy airplanes dangling from the ceiling, models in glass cases, photos and paintings on the walls and shelves full of aviation books.

Elsie threw her hands into the air. "The whole house is like this. Sometimes I feel like I'm running an aviation museum. Don't ever ask him what any of these things are—he'll *tell* you. Come on, the kitchen is in here."

A few minutes later Lorelei was drinking coffee out of a mug with a Spitfire on it. The old farmhouse-style kitchen overlooked the rocky spring flood of Teeter's Brook itself. Willow trees swept their branches through the bright water, flowers sparkled in Chris's overgrown gardens and the smell of damp, clean air reached her like a rare and perfect perfume. She and Elsie chatted until they grew comfortable with each other, and when the time came to leave, Lorelei was sorry she would *not* be enjoying any more of this sort of day. She drove off that afternoon with a carton of Odin mission photos, an office key she didn't plan to use and a wistful feeling she couldn't shake.

Over the next week, as summer got a firmer grip on the city, Lorelei made the trip to Teeterbrouck every day. On the weekend she simply suffered, not bold enough to wander around in Chris's house when Elsie wasn't there. The inconvenience plagued her—how would she be able to cope when the workload got really heavy? She had already run into trouble with the telephone situation. Messages were being left for her in Teeterbrouck, at her apartment and at Pioneer.

Elsie had no patience with what she considered nonsense. "When are you going to stop being so stubborn, girl? You've got to either move up here or move us down there."

"I know, I know. But let's wait for Chris to come back. I can't dump my stuff in his house without asking him."

"You're not dumping it in his house. This is an office—*Odin's* office."

"Well, still . . ."

Elsie glared. "He'll be back tomorrow."

"Promise you'll let *me* bring it up with him?"

"As long as you *do* bring it up."

"I will! I will!" Lorelei promised.

Lorelei knew she would have to keep her promise, but she managed to delay it for a couple of days, attending meetings in Manhattan and visiting printers. Elsie's phone call the second afternoon caught her in a rare moment at home. The emphasis in her dry voice told Lorelei just how annoyed she was. "Chris and I were just going over a few things, *now that he's back from St. Simon,* and I remembered that you *wanted to talk to him about something.*"

Lorelei sighed. "All right, Elsie, put him on."

She told herself she was ready to hear him, but his deep, resonant "Hello, Lorelei" poured into her like wine. It seemed to still be carrying the emotions of the last night on

St. Simon. Lorelei involuntarily closed her eyes and pictured him as he had appeared then...a powerful, confident man softened by hesitation as he had held her.

"Lorelei? Are you there?"

"Oh! Yes, sorry, my mind wandered—premature senility. I, um...Elsie is great, Chris. She's been a real help this past week."

"Yeah, I couldn't get along without her."

"I expect I'll get to that point, too. But I'm afraid I'm putting too much of a workload on her, asking her to keep track of the premiere stuff while I'm someplace else. It's turning out to be a problem, my working in the city and Odin's being based in Teeterbrouck."

"Is that so?" he inquired, brittle with caution.

"I think we need to consolidate."

"You mean you need to work up here."

"Yeah." There, it was out in the open. "I'll lease a car or something. The printer I've chosen is in Yonkers, and Howard and Deana work out of northern New Jersey, so it'll be more convenient for them, too." She shut up then so she wouldn't start babbling.

The silence before he answered seemed interminable. "Are you sure this is a good move?"

"It's a good *business* move."

"Business move—right. Give me some time to...make arrangements first."

What arrangements? Lorelei asked herself. Moving out of his house? "Fine. Let me know—whenever." She hung up before her voice broke.

The next morning the doorbell rang. She set down her first cup of coffee and stumbled downstairs. Chris stood on her tiny stoop, arms folded over a gray sweatshirt with the sleeves cut out of it, old jeans on his legs and ragged sneakers on his feet. He was glaring. No, she corrected, he was squinting from the sharp morning sunlight.

"Good morning. Jansen Freight Lines at your service."
He smiled.

Chris smiling at her? Lorelei decided she was still asleep.
Her dream even included a loud yellow rental truck parked
in front of her house. "Where am I moving to?"

"Teeterbrouck. Unless you've changed your mind."

"No. But . . . I thought you had some . . . arrangements to
make."

"I made them: the phone company is coming out to in-
stall another couple of lines, I rented a second desk and
typewriter, and I picked up this truck." He gave her another of his crooked smiles, reminding her of the first days
of their acquaintance. She had been able to enjoy his flirty
charm with a clear conscience then.

He frowned comically as she continued to stand there,
perplexed. Then he deliberately took gentle hold of her
shoulders, moved her to one side and stepped past her.

She came to her senses as he started up the stairs. "Chris!
Wait! Where are you going?"

"To pack," he called down. "Now you can either help or
I can put you in a carton and move you too."

Lorelei plunged after him and reached her apartment a
few steps behind. She looked around, seeing it as he must.
Oh, Lord, she thought, it looked like the inside of a trash
compactor. Her "pending" files were stacks of paper on
every flat surface; taped to lampshades and walls and the
edges of her desk were lists, catering menus, limousine es-
timates, reminders and messages. Piles of videotapes, old
movie posters, grant applications and Styrofoam coffee cups
lay everywhere else. At least the bed had been made.

"Chris, stop and talk to me for a minute!"

He put down a stack of folders and straightened. As she
watched, the forceful Chris who had barged into her home
so full of his own plans flickered unsteadily, and she realized that he was as nervous about his being there as she was.

"Do you still want to work up in Teeterbrouck?" he asked uncertainly.

"Well, I could definitely live without driving over the George Washington Bridge ten times a day, but...I thought..."

"That I wouldn't welcome you," he finished in a sad voice. "That you were better off working for Gilman. At least with him you knew where you stood, right?"

"Well..."

"I'm going to try very hard to prove I'm not a raving, demented maniac, Lorelei, really. I've never been involved in a big production like this, but I have the feeling you're going to be too busy to put up with any nonsense from a peculiar boss. So today I'm going to get you installed right where it makes the most sense for you to be, and then I'm going to quietly step out of your way. You won't even notice me."

In Lorelei's opinion, no project could get so overwhelming that she would fail to notice Chris, but she kept the thought to herself.

"So will you come up to Teeterbrouck?"

She studied him hopefully. Was he truly reconciled to her company? Was he perhaps the slightest bit eager for it? She couldn't tell. When he let his natural good humor shine out in this way he was irresistible. She couldn't trust herself to look past it, knowing how much she wanted to believe he was sincere. What choice did she have, anyway? She *needed* to work in Teeterbrouck, and he agreed.

"Let me go warn my landlady—she'll think I'm trying to slip out without paying the rent."

What did the director of a foundation do all day? If Lorelei had been unclear on this before the move, she soon got a detailed education. He talked to people—to students and faculties of medical schools, to executives at pharmaceutical companies and companies that made medical equipment. He spoke at conventions of health professionals, met with officials in the U.S. and abroad, exchanged information with liaisons from international health agencies and private nonprofit organizations. He was always on the road—or, more accurately, on the wing, flying off to exert his considerable charm on anyone who might help in Odin's work. If at first Lorelei had thought the Duchess an extravagance, she now realized it was as essential to Chris as an automobile was to her. Within a few days of the move she had bought an old bomb of her own and returned the Mercedes to her sister. She had her transport, and Chris had his.

Her fears about working too close to him began to seem like the fantasies of an overwrought girl. He was hardly ever there. Frequently after a business trip he drove to John Ward's house in Connecticut and skipped his own home entirely. When Lorelei needed his okay on promotional copy or his signature on a contract, the only sure way to find him was to lie in wait at the Teeterbrouck airport. Elsie claimed she did it herself.

Consequently, Lorelei found herself doing a lot of paperwork in the airport canteen. It almost defeated the purpose of the move, she told herself. Now Maggie had to take messages for her. But as the season advanced into June, she blessed every hour she spent away from the melting asphalt and airless streets of New York. For the first time since her childhood in the suburbs, summer seemed vividly beautiful, a drift of sultry days, perfumed by flowers and freshly mowed grass and spangled with fireflies at night. On the days Chris flew, she noticed the weather minutely, the changes in light, the patterns of the clouds, even the very texture of the air. While she knew she was far from "getting back in touch with nature," she *did* get great pleasure from knowing the phase of the moon and the exact time of the sunset.

Neither did the people she subcontracted to do various jobs seem to mind an occasional trip to the country. The graphic artists brought up their sketches and comps for her approval and then, before heading back to Manhattan, played games of badminton on the lawn. Howard and Deana spent three days rooting through the photo files looking for stills to include in their roughly cut documentary. Lorelei suspected they could have done it in less time had they left their bathing suits at home. Rosie herself spent whole days tanning in a lawn chair.

Chris made occasional appearances in his own home, wind-tousled from driving in the open Alfa. Each time Lorelei saw him, the gold of his skin was a little deeper, his hair a little blonder and his eyes a little more enigmatic. He always had a careless smile for her and an offhand comment about the work, but he invariably left her with the feeling that she'd had a door quietly closed in her face.

Most of the time she was able to shrug off her personal disappointment and go to him with small problems. But she knew the big problems would come soon enough and they'd be much harder to face him with.

The first one came at the end of June. One morning, as Lorelei stepped out of her clanking blue sedan, Elsie yelled through the office door, "I've got those Max Tech people on the phone again!"

"My lord, they *do* start early."

"Well, are you coming in to talk to them?"

"Uh . . . no. Tell them I'm not in yet."

Elsie complied, but was frowning in her stern parental way when Lorelei entered the office. "Are you feeling all right, Lorelei?"

"Oh, yeah, I'm fine. It's just . . . well, I haven't talked to Chris about this Max Tech business yet."

"Well, honey, get on it!" One of Elsie's most valuable and most annoying assets was her efficiency.

"Well, you know he's been busy, it's been hard to pin him down when he doesn't have something on his mind."

"All he's got on his mind right now is toast. He's in the kitchen having breakfast. Go on, scoot! You look like you could use another cup of coffee yourself."

Lorelei could think of no legitimate reason to put it off, at least none she could admit to Elsie. She threw a blouse on over the thin cotton shell she had worn for the heat and staunchly headed for the kitchen. The instant she pushed open the swinging doors she wished she hadn't listened to Elsie. At the big wooden table was not the sharp-eyed, sleek director of Odin, it was the private Chris. He had a soft, bleary quality about him that added another layer to his appeal—as if Lorelei needed to find one. He leaned his beard-roughened cheek on a hand, ostensibly reading a newspaper, but his eyes were half-closed. When he looked up, his expression was sweet. Oh, hell, she thought, a man who wakes up in a good mood. She herself woke sullen and fumbled everything she touched until she had drunk half a pot of coffee.

Her voice automatically dropped to a near-whisper. "Good morning, Chris. Sorry to break in on your muffin."

He looked to the plate that lay on the business section of the paper and seemed surprised to see it. "You know, I thought I dreamed making that muffin."

"Is that what you dream about—food?"

His lazy smile seemed rather more awake now. "Yeah, I'm a real sensualist."

Lorelei could think of no bland reply, so she changed the subject. "How do you feel about video equipment?"

"For breakfast?"

"As a sponsor for the premiere. You know the company Max Tech Electronics?"

"My CD player is a Max Tech."

"Well, I applied to their foundation for money, and they're interested. Real interested. They want to look at the rough cut of the documentary. I think we can get them to cover all the filmmaking costs."

Although he hardly shifted a muscle, wakeful energy seemed to course through him. "This sounds like something we should follow up on very carefully. You haven't *sent* them the documentary, have you?"

"No, I was kind of hoping you'd jump up and say, 'Lorelei, ask Max Tech if we can fly out and make a presentation in person.'"

"Oh, were you now?"

She searched his face for a sign that she had been pushy and found none. "Yeah, of course I was well prepared with hints to push you in that direction, but I don't take advantage of men who are half-asleep. I have my rules."

He looked interested. "I'd love to hear what they *are*."

She blushed and cleared her throat. "Max Tech's corporate headquarters are in Ann Arbor, Michigan. Maggie West showed me the local airports on a chart and—"

"Wait a minute! Wait a minute! I think I missed a cue back there."

She waited nervously, sure that she *had* been too forward this time.

"*Lorelei,*" Chris began theatrically, "*ask Max Tech if we can fly out and make a presentation in person....* Okay, now my role as leader is secure. Go make whatever arrangements you want."

"It's okay, then? We can fly out?"

He shrugged and pretended helplessness. "You and Elsie work out the schedule. I'll do whatever I'm told. I'm putty in your hands."

Interesting concept, Lorelei thought as she escaped. No one could control a Chris Jansen who had other ideas in mind, but one of the most winning things about him was that he could so cheerfully give up his autonomy when necessary. Tricks and manipulation didn't work with him; honesty did. All she had to do was convince him that an idea was good for Odin, and he adopted it with zest. As long as she only talked *business*.

The very next day, Lorelei was in the Duchess on her way to Ann Arbor. Flying seemed almost routine now. She realized she was beginning to accept it as a natural thing to do. As casually as she would pull into a highway rest stop, Chris set them down on a grass strip near Warren, Pennsylvania, and they ate a picnic lunch with the farmer who owned the field. They landed in Ann Arbor early enough to freshen up at their hotel and walk across the University of Michigan campus to Max Tech.

Although it was the summer session, the university town swarmed with kids. Lorelei had spent her professional life neck-deep in kids, and she noticed nothing strange. But Chris glanced around at the boys in shorts playing Frisbee on the flat green lawns and at the girls giving him stares of interest. He shook his head. "Boy, am *I* over the hill."

"What hill? You want to be eighteen again? *I* certainly don't."

"No, I suppose not," he agreed. "But you know, even during these past eight years of hobnobbing with doctors and executives and all the other respectable types, I've always felt sort of like the hobo at the edge of town. Here I look around and *I'm* the solid citizen, the old man. My self-image is crumbling."

He looked so tragic that she wanted alternately to comfort him and to hit him. "I hate to agree with you, but you *are* a solid citizen. But there's a strong hobo element in you, too."

"You're just saying that to be nice."

His smile didn't quite cover his genuine distress. Lorelei was perplexed. She had no trouble reconciling the two sides of his personality. She had always worked with people who had offbeat life-styles yet who kept up with their responsibilities and managed their careers very shrewdly. Rock mu-

sic was full of them. "Come on, you bum," she teased.
"Put on your respectable disguise, and we'll go coax wads
of money out of Max Tech."

"Right."

The meeting went without a hitch. It was a treat to sell the
premiere idea to people who were already three-quarters
sold. Lorelei showed the documentary, and Chris explained
the project. The two of them left the austere, scientifically
precise-looking Max Tech building certain they had found
their first major sponsor. To celebrate, they picked out a
campus greasy spoon for dinner.

"You watch," Chris observed over a slice of pizza.
"They're not only going to fund the entire documentary,
they're going to donate the on-board video equipment for
the next jet."

"You mean the camera in the operating room? The one
that films through the surgeon's microscope?"

"Yep, and all the monitors and headsets, everything. Expensive stuff, I know, but the brilliant Lorelei Chant just
handed Max Tech a million-dollar publicity gimmick: 'Max
Tech Electronics—precise enough to train a surgeon.'"

"Yeah, I guess I'm just an advertising genius."

Chris groaned. "I've created a monster."

"What? Did you like me better when I was humble?" She
immediately regretted her phrasing of the question. "Gil
kept me in line much better."

Chris caught her eyes and held them, more serious than
she felt was safe. "If you ever catch me doing *anything* Gil
did, I want you to tie me to one of the Duchess's propellers
and spin it out of me."

"I promise!" The peculiar exchange somehow left them
with a warm sense of camaraderie. Relaxed and pleased with
the way the day had gone, they walked back toward the hotel across the main campus square. Dozens of students
wandered and played under the streetlights. A boy in sus-

penders and clown trousers offered to teach them to juggle, but they escaped him, laughing.

"You should have tried it, Lorelei," Chris declared. "I'll bet you're a natural—your whole *job* is juggling."

"Are you telling me to switch careers?"

"And leave me at the mercy of my trustees again? No way."

She should have been flattered and pleased, but her heart unrealistically longed for more from him than professional admiration. *Stupid*, she told herself. Take what you can get, do your job, don't think about it. The more she concentrated on business, the better off she was.

"Last time I was here," Chris remarked, unaware of Lorelei's thoughts, "this place was full of anxious parents."

"What brought you to Ann Arbor? *This* place doesn't need free medical care."

"The medical school brought me. I was giving my pitch about starting a program whereby a student or two on financial aid could work it off over the summers by flying with Odin. It was just before the start of fall semester and all the new freshmen were wandering around trailing their parents, who looked like they thought they had just delivered their babies into the hands of the devil."

"What must your parents have thought when you went to Argentina?" The words had slipped out, and Lorelei couldn't believe she had said them.

Chris answered without flinching. "I hadn't been living with them for years by then. I left the minute I turned eighteen. But if I had been, they probably would have thanked the lord for getting me out of their hair. I was a wild kid. It was just a matter of time before . . . before I did something they couldn't bail me out of. I think they needed the peace."

"They must be pleased about how you turned out."

"I think they're still *waiting* for me to 'turn out.' They don't think this is a real job, you know—I'm still flying all over the universe, no wife, no kids. I don't even have a pet. Minnesota's a pretty conventional place. You live there with your feet planted firmly on the ground, none of this flitting around.''

Lorelei fell silent. She was beginning to understand him. Something in that rooted Minnesota life had so oppressed him that he had put half a world between himself and it. Even now, twenty years later, he still felt its tug like a deadly undertow, as if to stop swimming would be to drown. Yet he didn't seem to feel oppressed by Odin, and Lorelei couldn't think of a job with heavier responsibilities.

"Some flitting around,'' she teased him gently as they reached the hotel. "It's nine o'clock at night and I know very well you're going straight to bed. You're not even going to watch the news.''

"Gotta get up early, gotta be sharp to fly.''

"See what I mean? You've written a new definition for the word 'wild,' Chris. You really are an original.''

"So are you.'' He grinned.

Chapter Six

Whether Chris was a bum or a remarkable humanitarian or both in the same glorious package, the trip to Ann Arbor seemed to settle something for him. After weeks of all but ignoring Lorelei—except when she threw herself into his path—he was suddenly underfoot. He spent more time at home, and he sometimes even worked in the office with her, consulting her before she had to seek *him* out. He felt safe, she decided glumly. Evidently he viewed the trip as some sort of a test and was satisfied with its result—they had spent two days together, discussed personal subjects, worked as a team and nothing untoward had happened. It was a test Lorelei almost wished she had failed.

She felt like a woman with two personalities: the calm, competent one who viewed Chris as a business partner dominated when she forced it to, but the other one, the one that dissolved in a torrent of emotion when she saw him, lurked in the wings.

The work went well. While allowing that the worst was yet to come, she congratulated herself on the overall soundness of her plan. The documentary and half a dozen promotional spots were finished. Lorelei had booked the large, grand old Metropolitan Plaza in midtown Manhattan for the premiere and a room at the Waldorf for the party afterward. She and Chris had drafted reams of information about Odin, from photo captions to speeches for Rosie to six-panel brochures. The trustees had been coerced into approving the layouts for the printed material and the printer had begun work. Everything was organized and Lorelei enjoyed it, knowing it wouldn't last.

The first strains in the organization started to appear a week after her return from Ann Arbor. *The Veldt* won Best Picture at the Madrid Film Festival. Everyone who had been tepid about the project immediately heated up. The telephones started ringing at 8:00 a.m. when Elsie took them off night service and continued until she pulled the plug in the evening. Max Tech not only came through with funding for the documentary, they asked for Chris to come back to Ann Arbor and help them design the video equipment for a third jet, just as he had predicted. In addition, Odin was deluged with offers of sponsorship. Lorelei no longer had to beg. She turned her attention to negotiating with television networks.

It no longer bothered her to traipse about in Chris's house day after day. Even when he was home, he seemed to think of it more as a place to keep his airplane toys than as his private retreat. A man who lived more thoroughly through his job Lorelei could not imagine.

After weeks of working together, she finally felt comfortable enough with Elsie—or reckless enough—to ask her about it one day while they took an ice-cream break in the office.

"How can Chris stand to live Odin twenty-four hours a day, every day? Everyone associated with the foundation is very nice, of course, but doesn't he get tired of seeing them, talking Odin all the time?"

Elsie gave her a look of disbelief. "What are you talking about?"

"Um..." Lorelei struggled. "Well, you never find people dropping in to see him here. You know, people from town, friends. He doesn't have parties...." There was no way to go on without becoming too obvious.

Elsie stared at her. "You mean he seems to live like a monk? That he never goes out—never sees *women*?"

"Well..." Lorelei had meant exactly that, but she wasn't too sure she wanted to admit it.

Elsie reached for a stack of messages that awaited Chris's return from his latest trip and began to read them. "'Samantha Kane called. Please call her,' 'Evelyn Cimino—when will you arrive in Denver? Please call,' 'Grace Luned says next Friday is fine, can't wait to see you.' You want to hear more?"

Lorelei didn't. "Those are all women? I mean, I know they're all women, but...they're women he's going *out* with?"

"I just take the messages, honey. But think about it...a man like Chris?"

Lorelei thought about it frequently after that—every time a woman called who was vague about her business with Chris. There seemed to be dozens of them, scores of them. The lack of visitors in Teeterbrouck no longer lulled Lorelei into the sense that she had some kind of exclusive claim on him. She realized he had the perfect setup to live as a footloose playboy. With business and a plane to take him all over the globe, he could meet and fascinate any number of women. He would never have to settle on any one of them or worry that they would meet each other accidentally. And who could have refused him? Any woman worth her salt would feel flattered and thrilled to know Chris would call *her* when he was in her town.

As if they shared some sisterly psychic connection, Rosie

herself brought up the subject the very next time she and Lorelei met in the city for dinner.

"Look at us." She stabbed at her salad disconsolately. "Saturday night and not a man in sight. How are you doing with that beautiful man of yours, Lorelei?"

"He's not mine, if that's what you mean. I thought you understood that I was keeping this strictly business."

"Yuk. We can't really be sisters."

"Sure we can, you're just as professional when you want to be. No one will ever catch you mooning over someone you work with."

Rosie kept her eyes turned dismally to her plate and mumbled. "I don't know, hon. With some men it's not a matter of professionalism—it's life and death."

The melancholy note in her sister's voice caused Lorelei concern. "Does this have something to do with the man you came back to New York for? The one you won't tell me about? Oh, Rosie, he's not somebody on the film, is he?"

Rosie stopped her with a gesture. "I don't want to talk about it while it's still . . . pending."

"It *is* still pending?"

"I think so. Anyway, I'm treating it like that." She looked up with a rather manic smile. "Gosh, men are a bad subject for us, aren't they! Let's find another one. Who have you got on the guest list for the premiere party?"

Lorelei rattled off the names from memory: actors, musicians, critics, politicians, debutantes, noted spokesmen and champions of various good causes. Rosie's smile grew more and more luminous, and Lorelei cautioned her, "Now, none of these people has actually been invited yet, Rosie, let alone told us they're coming, so don't get your heart set on anyone."

"But you've got their phone numbers, right? You're going to call them?"

"I've got their agents' and managers' phone numbers. Anyone can get ahold of those."

"Hmm... We've got to do better than that. Can you give me a copy of the list?"

"Sure, but why?"

"I meet people! I *schmooze*. They say you're never more than—what is it?—five people away from anybody in the world. I'll bet I'm one person away from everyone on your list. I just have to get the old network going."

"Okay, I'll make a copy for you Monday."

"No sooner? I'm doing some heavy schmoozing tomorrow. Remember that rich alleged investment banker with the yacht?"

"The one you swore you'd never speak to again?"

"Yeah, him. He's giving a party on the yacht tomorrow. If I could have the list by then..." She grimaced in apology. "I've got to be at the dock in Oyster Bay by 10:00 a.m."

Ten! Lorelei despaired. She had so successfully transferred her office to Teeterbrouck that she didn't have a single copy of the list at her apartment. Chris was in Atlanta for the weekend or she would have considered asking him to read it to her over the phone. That would be a change from the way he was *probably* spending his Saturday evening, she thought—with Grace or Kitty or whoever he saw in Atlanta.

Rosie poked her with a carrot stick. "So? Can you get it to me?"

"I'll have to drive up to Teeterbrouck for it."

Rosie showed no trace of sympathy. "So? Drive."

"Oh, all right! I thought I could at least guilt you into offering me the Mercedes."

Her sister blinked and did not offer.

The trip was cursed from the beginning. No sooner had Lorelei pulled onto the West Side Highway than it began to rain. She splashed along in a stream of late-night traffic exiting Manhattan after the ballets and plays—all the things one *should* do on a Saturday night, Lorelei reflected, feeling the martyr. The forty-minute drive was stretched to an hour and a half. By the time she reached Teeterbrouck, the weather matched the tropical monsoons Chris had told her about. The hell with getting Rosie the list, she decided. She'd spend the night on Chris's sofa and float back in the morning.

At the foot of the serpentine driveway, the car began to jounce and jolt suspiciously. City girl though she was, she recognized the signs—she had a flat. Swearing proficiently, she pulled over onto the lawn, just in case someone swam up the driveway during the night and rear ended her. She turned off the lights, the wipers and the ignition and sat for a moment grinding her teeth. She told herself to be grateful the car hadn't broken down on the Palisades Parkway, but it was small comfort. There was nothing to do but get out and hike through the rain. Chris's house had warmth, lights, coffee and a phone. It even had dry clothes. She had stashed some outfits in the office closet for emergencies, though this wasn't the type of emergency she'd had in mind.

Hooking her key ring onto the belt loop of her cutoff shorts, she faced the rain. Chris's drive had turned into an inland waterway dotted with islands. She leaped from boulder to boulder, though it did little good. Her ponytail soon stuck to her back like a long piece of flypaper, and her tank top felt as if it had been fished out of a real tank. In the thin glare of the porch light she reached for the keys but found only the hook of the key ring. The keys had fallen off somewhere along the twisting, sodden driveway. Fine, she grumbled. In frustration, she kicked the door.

With Chris away, the house would be shut up like a safe. She rattled the doorknob without much hope. It was locked. Figuring she could hardly get any wetter, she began a survey of the ground-floor windows, willing to do *anything* rather than squish back down the driveway in the dark feeling for her keys. She floundered between the cold, slick shingles and the tough rhododendrons that crowded up against the house. Aha! One window stood open just a crack, a terrible breach of security in New York but perhaps not so bad in Teeterbrouck. She blessed Elsie for leaving it ajar and climbed onto a nearby rock.

The window led into the misnamed living room. Chris lived in it even less than he lived in the rest of the house. The pale blue sofa and the huge blue-and-white Oriental rug hardly ever felt a human touch. They'd feel one tonight, Lorelei remarked to herself. She was going to leave very human, very muddy footprints all over the rug.

She pulled back the flimsy screen and shoved the window farther open. Then she very carefully pulled herself over the sill belly first. She stuck wetly to everything, and her hair dragged at her head like a rope. With coordination that would not have gotten her a job in the circus, she crawled the last few inches, pulled her legs inside the window and dropped to her feet.

The next second, she hit the floor full length. A strong, massive weight had thrown her to the ground and now pinned her. She knew at once who it was—the feel of his flesh had been forever imprinted in her mind, along with the particular warm honey smell of his skin.

"Chris!" she cried breathlessly.

The hands that had wrenched hers over her head hesitated. One let go and a sudden brilliant light half blinded her; she had to turn her face away, eyes squeezed shut. Chris's familiar voice produced a rough stream of curses, and he pointed the flashlight in another direction.

"Oh, jeez, you're lucky I didn't *hit* you with this." He pulled himself up onto his elbows and glared at her, no friendlier a sight than the blinding dazzle of the flashlight. "Why are you breaking into my house in the middle of the night?"

"Practice?" she suggested. She knew she should have asked him to let her up; she could have managed a more intelligent answer if his chest hadn't been so close to her breasts. She could feel every breath he took, and his hard, muscular legs were alarmingly tangled with hers. But she didn't ask.

He growled something indecipherable and pushed himself backward. He rose, pulling her to her feet as well, and turned on a lamp. She looked down, trying to shield her night-focused eyes, and saw the condition she was in—covered with scrapes and splashes of mud, her top plastered to her like spray paint, dirty rainwater streaking down her bare legs. She was indeed making tracks on his carpet.

Her total disarray made her reckless. "So was Atlanta boring? Couldn't the Southern belles keep you there?" Lorelei was quite sure they had *tried*. If the night's prowl had left *her* a disaster, it hadn't hurt him a bit. He wore only loose pajama bottoms—no, she corrected herself, they were scrub pants, tied with a drawstring around his lean hips. The fabric was so fine she could see or imagine every contour of the body it covered. From the waist up he was a vision of perfect, tanned skin over the taut belly and broad, sleek chest she remembered once feeling beneath her hands. The sight of him left her weak and muzzy in the head—what had she just said? Something flip about women....

"You going to stand there making wisecracks while you catch pneumonia?" There was little sympathy in his voice.

"No... I guess I should explain. I drove up to get something from the office, but I had a flat down at the foot of your drive. I dropped my keys somewhere out there in the mud. Pretty disorganized for a producer, huh?"

"Yeah, not too impressive. You're lucky I'm *not* in Atlanta."

She braved looking up at him with an apologetic smile. "Oh, I don't know. I did get *in* all right. I could have called a garage and cleaned up the mud and gotten away with my reputation intact."

He looked far from amused. "Is the car off the road?" She nodded. "Then we'll deal with it tomorrow. I don't particularly feel like sitting in the mud changing a tire right now."

She flared. "You don't have to change it at all! You're the client, my problems have nothing to do with you. Go back to Atlanta, for heaven's sake!"

He gave her a look that could have stopped bullets, brusquely clamped his hand around her wrist and pulled her out of the room. By the time she got her feet under her again, he was dragging her up the stairs in the hallway. She had never been on the second floor before. She stumbled along after him, wondering if he planned to throw her out an upstairs window. In a bad movie he would have been taking her to bed, driven mad by passion. But she saw the wrong kind of passion in his iron grip and the hard, bunched muscles in his shoulders—it looked like anger. Surely he wasn't an abusive man, Lorelei told herself. He had reason to be annoyed, but he would never *hurt* her.

She dug in her heels at the top of the stairs, and Chris had to yank her the last few yards down the hall. The room he peremptorily threw her into was not his bedroom, it was his bathroom. As she stood witlessly on the cold tile floor, he reached into a closet, pulled out a mountain of white terry cloth and piled it on the edge of the sink. "Let's get rid of the mud, shall we?"

His use of the plural went no further than words. Giving her a final glare, he shut the door between them. His footsteps receded down the hall.

Lorelei caught her breath, feeling the sudden lack of his presence like a vacuum. Chill and reaction made her start to shiver. She had been expecting drama, and she had gotten a pile of bath towels. It should have been funny.

The bathroom was nearly the size of her whole apartment. The tile floor and white painted brick walls looked new, but the claw-footed tub, the deep sink and the brass towel racks were clearly original to the house. She wondered if he valued these old things for themselves or if he had simply never had time to replace them.

She stopped speculating, not sure how much time she had to wash up before he came back to check on her. The days of camaraderie had fooled her. Friendship could carry people through awkward episodes like this, but she and Chris did not have a friendship. They had high-pressure feelings that could be given no outlet; instead of friendship, they had touchy mistrust. The strength seemed to drain from her bones like water. Dully she pulled the curtains closed around the tub and turned on the shower.

When all the dirt had floated off, she dried with Chris's pristine towels and wrapped herself in a thick white robe that smelled like limes and laundry soap. Now what? she wondered bleakly. As soon as she opened the creaky, bathroom door, Chris's voice growled up from the floor below. "The guest room is all made up. Last door on the right."

She leaned on the polished oak railing and stared down into the bare little foyer. Chris's voice had come from the den. She opened her mouth to call back, to say she was sorry or wish him good-night or something, but her throat closed upon the words. She turned and scuffed her way to the last door on the right.

Chris sat alone in the dark, surrounded by the unseen shapes and colors of airplanes. They were the only obsession he had ever allowed himself, the only things that had seemed to offer freedom in his life rather than boundaries. He wished he had one of the usual vices—smoking or drinking or biting his nails. He would have liked to indulge in one of them rather than sit there suffering the betrayal of his own body. From the moment he had felt Lorelei beneath him, soft and vulnerable on the living-room floor, all he had wanted to do was to crush her close, weld her sweetness to himself somehow, kiss her until he forgot who he was. But he couldn't forget anything sitting in the den. Every nerve ending in his skin burned with memories of all the times he had ever touched her. Their clamor made him grit his teeth.

Without even closing his eyes, he could see a vivid picture of Lorelei as she must look in his cold, white guest room, in the big bed that was a little too hard. The blue guest sheets were still stiff from lack of use; her tender, freckled skin would sting, if her *bruises* didn't keep her awake by themselves. The memory of how he had grabbed her and pushed her around like a prisoner shamed him.

He should have stayed in Atlanta! He had been planning to, needing a respite from the tensions of Teeterbrouck. But Frances, a lovely woman who usually soothed and delighted him, had thrown him out. She had explained with peculiar female logic that while she didn't mind sharing him with two hundred other women—her own invented number—she refused to share him with *one*. She claimed to feel a distinct difference. He hadn't understood what she'd meant at first. What one? Then the truth had occurred to him...Lorelei was the one. Frances had seen it before he had.

After leaving Atlanta, he'd done something very stupid. He'd broken his first rule of survival in the sky and flown home with his mind in turmoil. Carelessness like that had killed many a pilot. But then again, he reflected, he might torment himself to death on the ground just as easily.

Neither the hot shower nor the utter quiet of the house, so different from her own city home, lulled Lorelei to sleep. At 5:30, after lying stiff as a board for hours, she got up, put on her still-damp clothes, sneaked out of the house and found the keys where they had washed into a rut. By the time Chris caught her, she had changed the tire. He looked as tired and irritable as she felt.

"What the hell are you doing? Why didn't you wait for me?"

"Didn't want to impose," she answered airily. "You probably would have been gallant and insisted on changing the tire yourself."

Her sarcasm clearly stung him. "I would have called a mechanic. There are people who get paid to do this stuff—as you so astutely pointed out."

"Yeah, well, you're paying me to organize your fundraiser, not to complicate your life with car trouble." Or any other kind, she added privately. "Besides, I have to meet my sister early today. Go back to bed, it's Sunday. Have a doughnut, read the paper." She swung herself onto the front seat and closed the door between them; the gesture echoed the one he had made the previous night when he had left her in the bathroom. That was evidently to be the tone of their relationship from now on, she decided, irritation and as much distance as possible.

"Lorelei!" he called harshly. But she had released the brake and started to back down the lumpy driveway. To his credit, Chris sprang ahead and checked the road for cars before she backed out into it, but his mouth was set in a tight, hard line. She straightened herself in the road and drove on without looking back.

She turned over the list to Rosie in an ill temper and escaped before her sister could conduct a third degree. The only comment Rosie got out was a heartfelt "My, you're a mess!" And wouldn't you be, Lorelei asked her silently, after changing a tire at 6:00 a.m. to escape from a man who couldn't wait to be rid of you?

After she had showered and changed in her own apartment, Lorelei still felt a mess. Worse, she felt intrinsically unattractive, as if her skin gave off some unwholesome pheromone that made her poisonous, particularly to Chris Jansen. It wasn't fair! she protested to her unsympathetic mirror. She hadn't thrown herself at him. In fact, literally speaking, it had been quite the reverse—a point she should have found funny but didn't. From the very beginning, she had *tried* to keep her feelings to herself, and she had *still* ended up in his arms twice. She had tried very hard to accept the fact that he had no use for her as a woman, but he made it difficult to keep that in mind. And now she was blaming herself, even hating herself for causing such problems.

Rosie called her at noon from the yacht. The sounds of a live band and an even livelier party made a heart-to-heart talk impossible.

"You're not working, are you, Lorelei?" Rosie yelled.

"Goodness, no. Chris Jansen has not bought me body and soul." Not that he'd needed to, Lorelei reminded herself. At one time he could have had either for the asking. "How goes the jet set?"

"Well, it's kind of novel to be the center of attention rather than a fringe element the way I usually am. Everyone's asking about the movie. I'm making some progress on your list, too."

"Good."

"But I'm not going to let you talk about work on your Sunday off. What fun things have you got planned?"

Lorelei stared at the barren apartment, stumped. At that moment she had been sitting on the floor looking at the dust bunnies under the couch and wondering if she should just let them stay there. "Oh, I don't know.... Actually, I'm in kind of a rotten mood."

"Oh?" Rosie had the grace to sound surprised.

"What do you do when you feel like a total waste of life?"

"That's easy—I blow money. I get my hair done, I buy clothes, I eat out and drink lots of wine...actually I drink so the hairdresser's bill doesn't bother me. You know, come to think of it, you could use a trim. Do you want Raymond's phone number?"

Lorelei wrote it down, thinking that she hardly felt up to the ultracool of Rosie's favorite salon. If she felt ugly in her own apartment, she'd surely feel like a toad with a smock tied under her chin.

An hour later, as Raymond massaged shampoo through her hair, she decided she felt great, no matter how she looked. Raymond adored women; he had strong fingers and a soft voice and flattered her shamelessly. She had a trim, a manicure and a facial and drank two glasses of the salon's wine.

There was little time left to buy clothes after she left—and even less money left in her budget—but Lorelei was determined to follow her sister's advice to the letter. She picked a boutique she had long admired—from a safe distance—announced to a salesgirl that she had come in to cheer herself up and took over one of the ivory-silk dressing rooms. An hour and a half later she walked out with five new outfits. She did feel better, she realized—impoverished but better. She had never indulged herself so; the Lorelei Chant she was used to worked hard and put up with things. Chris Jansen had really knocked her off stride. If she didn't find an antidote to him, she would surely end up in debtor's prison.

The next morning she put on one of her new outfits, a graceful linen sheath the same unbearable blue as Chris's eyes. She took special care with her braid and the small amount of makeup she used. She decided she looked great, as good as the Lorelei that Gil had hauled out to decorate his side at parties, but softer, more classic. She had always thought that avant-garde styles helped give her baby-faced features more sophistication, but she saw now that it wasn't so. The more subdued Lorelei turned out to have a timeless look, a sleek, well-groomed refinement. Confidence welled through her. To hell with gas mileage! she told herself recklessly. With the car's feeble air-conditioning cranked up to high, she might just make it to Teeterbrouck in good condition.

On her way to the car, her high spirits began to sink. Facing Chris from now on, day after day, would take more confidence than she could get from a new dress or a pair of earrings. She thought wistfully of all the liberties she had taken when she'd needed his attention, the times she had waited at the airport or handed him wrenches and talked things over while he worked on the Alfa. Her senses always sparked near him, and her awareness of him was so keen it hurt. But still there had been a sort of working ease between them, a naturalness about dealing with Odin's problems together. Yet all those days and weeks of workaday partnership had done nothing to kill the stronger currents between them.

What would she do now, with their relationship in such a shambles? The answer came to her—*Sylvia*. Lorelei hadn't planned to hire assistants until the workload became unbearable, but it seemed to have just become so.

Relieved, Lorelei dialed Gil's still-familiar phone number. Sylvia herself answered. She sounded tense and harassed, not at all her usual giddy self. Gil's employee relations had apparently not improved. Lorelei dispensed with formality. "Sylvia, how'd you like to come work for me in Teeterbrouck?"

The girl broke down in tears. "Oh, Lorelei, I'd mop floors for you. I'd mind your children! Anything to get out of here."

"Good. Now, I know you'll want to give a couple weeks' notice...."

"Notice?" Sylvia wrestled with the idea. "I suppose that would be the civilized thing to do. But you know very well no civilized deed goes unpunished around here."

Lorelei wanted to agree. For Sylvia to start immediately would please her very much, but a stubborn sense of ethics kept her silent.

"You still there, Lorelei?"

"I'm still here."

"Well, when can you pick me up and get me to Teeterbrouck?"

"Are you sure, Sylvia? Don't you want to think about it a little?"

"Heck, no. If I think about it, I'm bound to think of some meaningful parting gesture, if you know what I mean. No, the quicker you come get me, the safer Gil will be."

An hour later Lorelei picked up a buoyant, bubbling Sylvia from the sidewalk in front of her old office building.

"I don't want your conscience to bother you, Lorelei. My quitting now won't be as bad as you think. Gil took on a new assistant after you left and she suits him—she's a real killer. Plus, we're between concerts. We've just been sitting around drinking too much coffee and trying to dig gossip out of each other. Gil will only miss me like he'd miss a chair that gets in his way."

"Don't underestimate him. The day Gil Gilman is magnanimous about anything is the day I leave the business."

"I guess you're in it for the duration, then. No, really, Lorelei, Gil won't even care that I've left. Now fill me in on this Odin business. Wait! This is the foundation run by that gorgeous man—the one I gave the pass to last year! Oh, right! You know, when I read in the trades that you had snagged the project, I remembered it was the one Gil had wanted, but I didn't make the connection with Chris Jansen. Oh, I'm in heaven!"

Lorelei envied Sylvia her simple enthusiasm. Time enough for that to fade on its own, she thought as she explained the project. As giddy and silly as Sylvia could be at times, she paid careful attention, making notes, remembering names and identifying the tasks she could best take on herself.

A hopeful calm returned to Lorelei. She hadn't realized what a strain it had been running the whole show alone. Elsie had been a help, but Sylvia knew the business and had been fire-tested under Gil. More to the point, Sylvia would be a buffer between her and Chris.

Lorelei drove her new assistant through Teeterbrouck, showing her the post office, the stationery-supply store and the all-important late-night deli. When a large commuter bus passed them on the narrow main street, Sylvia lit up. "Hey, you know, I think Teeterbrouck is on the same bus route as Nyack—I live in Nyack. This is going to be a heck of a lot more convenient than dragging myself down into Manhattan every day."

"Good. I'll let you hold down the fort here, and since I've got the car I'll do the running back and forth." With any luck, Lorelei thought, she'd hardly ever run into Chris. She knew it was the coward's way out, but she hadn't the guts for anything else. She *was* a coward.

"There's one other place you should see, Sylvia—the airport. You'll probably be spending a lot of time out there waiting for Chris. It's his second home."

"Waiting for him won't be much of a hardship," Sylvia said dreamily. When Lorelei didn't reply, she frowned.

At the airport, Lorelei balked. Chris's battered Alfa sat in the parking lot. She hadn't expected him to be there. But she parked, knowing she'd have to face him eventually— better now while she was fresh and had Sylvia with her. They found Maggie in the house manning the Unicom. She looked up long enough to tell them that they'd come just in time; another fifteen minutes and Chris would have taken off.

Taken off? Lorelei was puzzled. Did he have appointments today? She couldn't remember any. Steeling herself, she led Sylvia out to the apron of blacktop between the hangars and the runway. The familiar shape of the Duchess shone in the sunshine, white as soap. Its propellers were turning, and the pilot made a dark shape behind the tinted windshield. As they approached, the props slowed and the engine noise died. Chris jumped down to meet them. Even behind his wire-rimmed glasses his eyes looked stormy. Could Sylvia notice it? Lorelei wondered, or was the glower for her alone?

"Chris, sorry to pluck you out of the sky like this." Was that *her* voice? Lorelei wondered. It sounded so normal. "But we were in the area, and I wanted you to meet my new assistant. Actually, you did meet her months ago in Gil's office. Sylvia Torres—Chris Jansen."

She watched the two exchange pleasantries, feeling as if she was waiting for a bomb to go off. It never did. Chris was charm itself, as usual, and Sylvia was too enchanted with him to notice Lorelei's discomfort. When the introductions were over, Lorelei found herself remarking pointedly, "I don't recall Elsie mentioning that you had any flying plans today. I thought you liked to get a couple days' rest between trips."

"Is there any pressing work that I should stay for?" he asked carefully.

"No, nothing that can't wait if you have business elsewhere."

"This is a pleasure trip," he said, looking her straight in the eye. "To Cape Cod."

Embarrassment stabbed through Lorelei like a hot spear. A pleasure trip to Cape Cod, huh? Without any effort at all she remembered the name of a woman who left messages for Chris with a Massachusetts area code. "Oh," she said stiffly. "Then we won't keep you another minute. Have a safe flight." She turned and stalked away so abruptly that Sylvia gave a little cry of exasperation. Lorelei heard the girl gasp out a quick "Goodbye, nice to meet you again!" before scrambling to follow.

By the time they reached the car, the Duchess's engines had spun to life again and could be heard as a low, throaty hum, a much softer growl than Lorelei imagined she'd heard in Chris's voice.

Sylvia threw herself hurriedly into the car, as if afraid her boss would drive off without her. "Um ... Lorelei?"

"Yes?" Lorelei answered in a tone she hoped would discourage any probing questions.

"Is ... er ... is Chris a hard man to work for?"

"No, you won't have any problems, Sylvia." She gave a heavy sigh. "It's just me."

Chapter Seven

August and September were just cool enough that Lorelei could make the drive in and out of Manhattan as frequently as she needed to and not look like a rag at the end of each trip. She dressed well even when no one would see her but Elsie and Sylvia. She made sure no detail of her appearance ever caused her to cringe in front of a mirror. Of course, she knew very well what her clothes had become to her—armor. She was protecting herself from Chris. No matter what he thought of her or how he behaved toward her, no matter how she seemed to be falling apart inside, she would at least be able to look at herself in a mirror and see a well-put-together young professional woman who was good at her job.

One morning, as she and Sylvia put stamps on the premiere invitations, she realized that her preoccupation with the private drama between herself and Chris was effectively keeping her from worrying about the premiere. "Sylvia, take my temperature. I just addressed envelopes to the governor of New York and three of my favorite actors, and I didn't even feel a thrill.''

"It's when you make the follow-up personal phone calls that you'll get the full effect," Sylvia reassured her.

"I guess..." But Lorelei guessed the opposite. In order to finalize the deal to broadcast the documentary and parts of the premiere, she had been to dinner the previous week with executives from one of the major television networks. Yet, except for the business talk itself, she had barely paid attention to the conversation. Chris had been scheduled to fly that evening, but it had stormed ferociously and she had been sick with worry that he would be caught in it. How could she continue to operate on such a high level with half a brain? she wondered. Did other people do it?

She snapped her thoughts back to the present when she realized Sylvia was looking at her suspiciously. Sylvia had shouldered a great part of the project, but she still seemed to have a lot of energy left over to poke into Lorelei's personal affairs. Lorelei often felt herself under scrutiny, particularly when Chris was involved, either in the flesh or merely in conversation. She knew the girl had not accepted a word of her bland explanations about how well they got along. It was obvious to everyone that she and Chris did not have a normal business relationship.

Elsie kept her own counsel, but Sylvia was different. Lorelei told herself she should have expected problems. Sylvia's talk had always been chock full of saucy gossip— who had married, divorced or been seen with whom. And she'd always teased Lorelei about her monkishness. She thought everyone's life could be spiced up with a little romance, and she seemed to consider herself a sort of freelance cook. For two weeks she'd been watching Lorelei with a look of speculation. Sooner or later, Lorelei knew, Sylvia would say something she didn't want to hear.

But would *Chris* ever say anything? Elsie complained that he prowled about the house like a restless lion, making her and Sylvia jumpy with his moods. Lorelei knew for herself that his temper had become very unpredictable. Sometimes he seemed as serene as a sleeping cat and other times he flared like a struck match. His dark, observant eyes flashed messages at her that she preferred not to read, and she'd adopted a sharp, peppery tone in order to keep the catch out of her voice. She couldn't bear to let him see how he affected her.

One day in mid-September, her acting ability took a severe beating. Chris slouched in the chair by her desk pretending to be absorbed in his appointment book while she leafed intently through hers. They were trying to find a free space in his schedule after he came back from his imminent trip to Rochester so he could rehearse Rosie in her speeches for the premiere.

The telephone rang, and Sylvia picked it up in the adjoining office, then stuck her head through the doorway and announced in a dire voice that Gil wanted to speak to Lorelei.

That's all I need, Lorelei commented to herself sourly. She would rather have heard that every known copy of the movie had been lost than talk to him. Under Chris's watchful eyes, she picked up the phone. "Hello?"

"Is this Miss Chant—*the* Miss Chant, renowned East Coast producer?"

"Hello, Gil. What can I do for you?"

"Oh, you've done quite enough already, sugar. Enough to keep my lawyers busy for months."

"What are you talking about?" She forced herself to sound bored, but the bottom of her stomach had started to churn.

"How's stealing my account for starters? How about stealing my employees? You and that nitwit Torres deserve each other, but trading on the trust I put in you, using inside information to steal the Odin account... I'm afraid even a man of my good nature can't let that pass."

"Don't be ridiculous, Gil. You know very well that's not what happened."

Chris's gaze had sharpened, though he couldn't possibly decipher Gil's words from where he sat.

"I don't know any such thing, sweetie. On the contrary, the whole thing looks damn fishy. As I think back on our last delightful days together, I remember how *cozy* you were with our boy Jansen. You got along like a house on fire, in fact. Innocent, trusting soul that I was, I never considered the possibility that you were manipulating the both of us. It wasn't any coincidence that he rejected my proposal and then, two seconds later, you quit and started your own business."

"I thought you fired me, Gil."

Gil ignored her sarcasm. "Just what did you offer him to get the job for yourself? You want me to spell it out for you, you and your Miss Prim act?"

"Very flimsy, Gil. Why are you wasting your time on garbage like this? Is business that slow for you?"

"Not so flimsy that I can't make life hell for *you*, sister. No one steals my clients and my employees and tries to take over my action in the Northeast."

"You sound like you've joined the mob or something."

"This is a rough business, honey. And I'm going to show you just how rough it can get."

"Nice try, Gil." She hung up calmly and put her hands in her lap behind the desk; she didn't want Chris to see how they had begun to shake. Did Gil have anything? she wondered. Enough to interest a judge? She had no doubt the scurrilous lawyers he retained would pursue any case he sent them. How much damage could they do to her before they got it to a judge? Gil's point was obviously to rattle her during the final, critical weeks of the project. He had succeeded. She didn't dare open her mouth to speak lest her voice shake as her hands were shaking.

"Lorelei?" Chris's voice held a soft note of concern. "Is something wrong?"

"No, Gil's just wishing me luck in his own inimitable way. He's such a sweetheart." She knew she hadn't fooled Chris a bit. The tiny muscles around his eyes and mouth had tightened in suspicion. Still, he didn't press her. That, more than his past tempers and stiff silences, made her sad. For a time—such a short time, it seemed—he had been the strong, sympathetic friend to whom she could have turned with a problem like this. He would have gotten very satisfyingly enraged at Gil, then wrapped her in his warm humor and refused to let her worry. She sighed involuntarily, then went briskly back to arranging his schedule.

Chris found himself banging through the upstairs like a storm wind, stomping across the hardwood floors, slamming doors, yanking out bureau drawers and throwing clothes into his suitcase. He sat down on the bed to get a grip on himself. He was acting like a sulky kid who had decided to run away from home. Very mature, he told himself. He was just supposed to be packing for a business trip, an operation he had performed scores of times. He had already done his running away from home at eighteen.... He had packed a knapsack and hitchhiked past the fields of winter wheat to the airport at Thief River Falls, Minnesota. There he had earned board and flying time by washing and fueling the aircraft of a small commuter line. From then on, he had been as free as a bird—literally—flying roundups, charters and fire patrols, working as a line boy and sleeping in hangars when money got low. Somewhere along the way, he had signed on with Odin and bought a house, but he still had the life-style he liked. What did he have to run from?

Lorelei, that's what. Sometimes it seemed she was going out of her way to agitate him. He lived in constant suspense, never knowing when he'd see her, unable to either put her out of his mind *or* get used to her. She'd be absent for days on end, then turn up looking elegant and alluring—and so aloof! Where was the sweet ragamuffin he had first met? He never knew when to brace himself to see her and when to let down his guard; he was jumpy twenty-four hours a day.

Footsteps creaked down the hallway toward him and paused in the doorway. Heart tripping, Chris snapped his head around. "Lorelei?" But it wasn't Lorelei, it was her dark, curly-haired assistant Sylvia. If Chris had ever thought Lorelei painfully young, compared to Sylvia she seemed like the very rock of maturity and reason. Sylvia was as apt to giggle as to speak.

"No, it's Sylvia. Sorry to walk in on you."

"Skip it. Do you need me for something?"

"Lorelei wants to know if you can stay an extra day in Rochester and see this fellow who claims he's written a theme song for Odin."

Chris sighed. Lorelei wanted to know, but she had sent Sylvia to ask. At least Sylvia looked uncomfortable about being the proxy—and rather sympathetic. *Very* sympathetic, Chris realized. Could he trust her? He was seriously tempted. Could he ask her what Lorelei thought of him, why she was tormenting him with her prickly, reproachful manner? Their relationship had been so nice and uncomplicated before she had climbed in his window the night of the storm. He had almost convinced himself that they made a good team and that he'd come out of their stint together unscathed.

His heart demanded too much from him; it thundered with the fury of all he needed to say to Lorelei—and couldn't. He looked at the juvenile face of her assistant and knew he must be skirting madness. To consider confiding in this light-witted child was lunacy.

Why was she standing in front of him now? He struggled to remember. Something about a man with a song in Rochester.... "Tell her I'll do whatever she wants me to."

Sylvia smiled brilliantly and prepared to go.

"Sylvia, what did Gilman call about?"

"She didn't tell you?"

"No. She . . . she doesn't like to bother me with problems she thinks she can handle." That was quite true, he reflected. It would probably pass as an answer. "But I don't have a very good opinion of your former boss. If he's bothering her about something, I want to know what."

He had struck a responsive chord in Sylvia. "I'm with you. He'll cause her trouble if he possibly can. But she didn't tell *me* anything, either."

"Hmm . . ." He flashed her his most endearing smile, the one that seemed to make women want to do things for him—every woman, that was, except Lorelei. "While I'm in Rochester, see if you can find out, okay? Lorelei doesn't need to carry all these worries alone."

"Sure thing, boss." Sylvia glowed, clearly delighted to be part of his conspiracy. Perhaps, Chris thought, he had been a little harsh in his judgment of her. Not everyone could measure up to Lorelei.

While Chris was north courting a Rochester pharmaceutical company, Lorelei made a trip south. She had needed to spend a couple of days with her still photographers getting pictures of one of the Odin jets, and when the eye hospital flew to Miami for repairs, she hurried down to catch it. She also arranged a meeting with a medical school that wanted to send two of its illustrious professors up to the premiere. Lorelei had decided to check them out before bothering Chris. She took Sylvia along to give her a little field experience.

It should have been a vast relief to travel with Sylvia rather than Chris. Unfortunately, Lorelei discovered that the quiet harmony she had found with Chris, the sense of sharing a purpose and of not having to constantly discuss it, was not duplicated. After two nights in a hotel with Sylvia, the little personality quirks that had seemed only mildly bothersome before were becoming incentives to kill. The girl could not shut up, could not close up shop at the end of the day and entertain herself. She liked to chat, particularly about personal things, and she seemed to consider the trip one long slumber party arranged to talk over old times.

"Gosh, the tension level in that office was so high you could get a nosebleed from it. Remember? Gil must have fought with everyone he did business with."

"No," Lorelei corrected. "Just with everyone he thought he had some power over. He fawned over the bigwigs." She huddled deeper inside her sweater and stared out at the eerily lit hotel pool. She had turned the air conditioning to frigid levels, hoping to drive the thin-blooded Sylvia back to her own room.

Sylvia sprawled on one of the beds, flipping the cable-TV channels with the sound turned down and eating peanuts from the hall vending machine. "That's true. No wonder his expense account was so high. And his *lawyer's* fees—from suing the living daylights out of every poor slob who ever crossed him! Gil the Merciless. I'd hate to be on the wrong side of Gil Gilman."

Lorelei sighed. She knew what this was all about. Sylvia had been trying to find out why Gil had called her in Teeterbrouck. Lorelei rarely let herself get talked, tricked or pressured into anything, but her resistance was wearing down. Perhaps Sylvia had a right to know, she rationalized. Gil might very well suck her into the case if it ever came to court. "You're already on the wrong side of him."

"Oh, you mean by quitting and coming to work for you?"

"Yeah. I've become one of the poor slobs he's suing. He claims I stole the Odin account." There, she had told someone. Why didn't she feel any better? Because, she admitted to herself, she hadn't told Chris.

Sylvia sat up suddenly, peanuts tumbling in all directions. "You're kidding! You didn't steal Odin! Did you?"

"Of course not! I'm not even doing a rock concert for them, so the whole thing is just ridiculous. Gil's just trying to keep my life interesting."

"As if any life around Chris could be dull...." Sylvia barely noticed the glare this comment pulled from her boss. "So what's the rest of the story?"

"The rest?"

"Yeah—the gory details. Gil must have something more specific. I mean, is he claiming you bribed Chris to give you the job or something?"

"In a manner of speaking...."

"In a manner of—" Sylvia abruptly shut up. Whatever had just occurred to her had shocked her into a few seconds of speechlessness. But only a few. "You mean—is he accusing you of sleeping with Chris to sell your proposal?"

Lorelei looked away. "That's about the size of it."

"What a jerk!" Sylvia was silent again, this time for a suspiciously long time. When she spoke again, her voice was extremely hesitant. "He doesn't...er...have a case, does he?"

"Sylvia!"

"Sorry! Sorry! It's just...I mean...I don't know what I mean."

"Evidently," Lorelei agreed coldly.

"Aw, Lorelei, give me a break. You can't tell me things are exactly...ordinary between you and Chris. Sometimes I feel like the demilitarized zone in a war between the two of you. I don't know where the mines are planted, what to say, when to run for cover. When Gil was going after the account, I thought you and Chris were getting along fine from the way you talked about him. Now, I don't mean I thought that anything was *going on*."

Lorelei folded her arms over her chest and sank back into her seat, letting Sylvia continue.

"Okay, maybe I *hoped* something might be going on."

"Oh, *did* you?"

"Yeah, I thought I detected some chemistry there."

"Well, life's just a little more complicated than chemistry, Sylvia—people have other concerns, they make choices." Like Chris's choice to be a loner, Lorelei added silently.

Sylvia looked dashed. "I suppose so. But I wouldn't have thought there'd be any choice with Chris. I mean, *look* at him. *I'd* take him in a second."

It suddenly occurred to Lorelei that Sylvia thought *she* had refused *Chris*—a flattering revelation, but so far from the truth it made her laugh. The laugh had a wild edge to it. For a long time she had been so smug, believing that she had conquered her romantic longings. But, had the choice really been hers to make, would she have rejected Chris? Not likely, she thought.

As soon as Lorelei looked up and noticed an uncertain half smile on Sylvia's face, she sobered. "Sorry, Syl, I wasn't laughing at you. It's just...never mind. Listen, I haven't told Chris about Gil."

"Yeah, I guess it's not the kind of thing you'd just casually mention."

"Good, you understand. We'll let this blow over by itself."

Sylvia nodded energetically. "Yeah, I've never seen Chris really angry, and I'm not sure I want to."

But despite their pact, when they returned to Teeterbrouck, Chris *was* angry. Lorelei and Sylvia walked in together, having taken a very early plane from Miami and driven up in Lorelei's car. They found Chris sitting on Lorelei's desk, his dark, slanted gaze focused on her. He began without preamble. "I've always admired your ambition, Lorelei. But since when did you take over as Odin's medical liaison?"

It took her travel-weary brain a moment to figure out what he meant—oh, yes, the professors she had gone to see.

They had been an aggravating bunch, and Chris should have been grateful she had taken them off his hands. She dragged herself tiredly to her chair and sat down. "Since medical schools decided their professors needed to hobnob with the glitterati."

Chris hopped off the desk and confronted her with a glare. "As talented and bright as you are, Lorelei, as much as you've learned about this operation over the past few months, you are *not* a medical expert. You just don't have the answers people expect if Odin is going to maintain its rigorous reputation."

"Of course I don't," she agreed. Through the dark cloud of his criticism, she caught the gleam of something wonderful—he thought her talented and bright! He had said those words without a trace of sarcasm. But still the slur on her judgment stung. "Chris, if I had thought those guys had legitimate medical questions, I would have handed them over to you on a silver platter. But they just wanted to have their photos taken with Rosie for the walls of their waiting rooms. Since when do you waste your time with idiots?"

"Since day one, Lorelei. Odin is my responsibility—idiots and all. I'd appreciate it if you'd let *me* decide who qualifies. I do not need someone to protect me."

"I'm sorry! I'll send you some of *my* idiots to make up for it, okay?"

His reply sounded like the warning rumble of an earthquake, but he stalked out of her office before he did any damage. Lorelei shuffled papers for a while, wishing desperately that she had not lost her temper. It was cowardly to hide behind sarcasm. She wondered when she had last been truly nice to him. Eons ago, back when they had gotten along. Every tart remark that left her mouth proved how right he was to want her out of his life. He had a naturally sunny disposition, but Odin was a demanding mistress. He had to raise its budget single-handedly and spread its reputation with skill and charm. He didn't need Lorelei adding to his burden.

She had talked herself into a very contrite attitude by the time the office door opened. Chris's tall, quiet figure appeared. Sylvia cleared her throat, and Lorelei looked up from a batch of contracts. Chris smiled sheepishly. She smiled back; it was hard not to smile at Chris.

"I came to say thank you for your protection." His voice was low but fervent. "I realized we've both got more than our share of idiots to deal with, and I'm one of yours."

Lorelei flushed with pleasure. This was no shallow apology slapped together just to appease her. She knew very well Chris had been brooding ever since he had left her.

"It's okay," she said. "There are rewards. That same idiot is talented and bright and has worked very hard these past few months to learn about *my* operation."

The creases in his cheeks deepened and the heartiness returned to his voice. "Well, idiocy is probably one of my permanent character flaws, but for now I'm going to plead overwork—for all of us—because I've got a treatment for that."

"Oh, yeah? What?"

Chris sauntered around the desk and pulled her to her feet. He kept his hand on her just long enough to push her toward the door; then he scrupulously let go. "You'll see. Break time, team," he roared into the next room. "Elsie, come on out here."

The woman emerged and frowned at her boss. Sylvia looked from Lorelei to Chris and back again in perplexity.

"Chris, what are you doing?"

"*We*, Lorelei. *We're* taking the afternoon off. It's fall in the Hudson Valley. The leaves are changing, the apples are getting picked, the doughnuts are frying."

"Doughnuts?" Lorelei repeated.

Elsie's gaunt face beamed with comprehension; she grabbed her scarf from the coatrack. "You know, in all the frenzy lately, I completely forgot about the doughnuts. Just let me turn the phones over to the answering service and we can go."

Lorelei decided that Elsie had caught the same mental illness as Chris. "*What* doughnuts? Have we gone into the baking business or something?"

"Nope," Chris said triumphantly, shoving her out the door. "The eating business. This is an inviolable Odin tradition. Every fall Elsie and I drive up into the orchards to the cider mill for cider and fresh doughnuts. Actually, we do it a little more than once a season."

"More like once a week." Elsie gathered up Lorelei's jacket and thrust it at her. Sylvia, never one to miss a chance for fun, had already run outside toward the cars.

"But we've got work to do," Lorelei protested. "Calls coming in..."

Elsie had no use for her complaints. "And an expensive answering service that can very well earn its money."

Lorelei looked back to Chris, who had put on a hurt face. "Now, Lorelei, I'm trying so hard to prove I'm a better boss than Gilman. You're not going to shoot down my timid little attempt, are you?"

"Timid?" She felt herself being gently herded out into the crisp fall air and saw him lock the door behind him. "Kidnapping is timid?"

"Don't forget grand theft auto. We're taking your car."

"You've never driven my car; it's strange, it..."

"So *you* drive it. Far be it from me to get between a lady and her car."

Just feeling flippant, Lorelei asked, "What about your macho image?"

Chris stumbled to a halt and screwed his face into the most pathetic expression Lorelei had ever seen. "Macho? Me?"

Sylvia doubled over with giggles; even Elsie smirked. But Lorelei stood firm. "Yeah, you know—the stalwart pilot facing the cold impersonal heavens all alone, all that stuff."

"Is that the impression I give?" He looked mystified; then a grin blossomed on his face, and he puffed out his chest. "Gosh, I guess I am kind of dashing, aren't I?"

Lorelei shot him a quelling look. "Well, dashing or not, I don't have any macho reputation to maintain, and since I don't know where we're going, *you* drive."

Though it was cold, they opened the windows so they could smell the tang of fallen leaves and wood smoke. Chris whipped the car over the twisting country roads, rock-steady at the wheel. Lorelei ceased worrying about her car's quirks; Chris seemed to have tamed them.

The hills were a collage of toasted orange and gold, and the cold barb of winter blew in on the northwesterly wind. How had fall sneaked up on her? Lorelei wondered. Up here in Chris's hills, she had been keenly aware of summer. When had she lost touch? The answer depressed her—it had been when she had lost touch with Chris. She had become preoccupied with staying out of his way, spending long days in the city, phoning in her instructions to Sylvia. The summer had faded without her being there to see it.

It took barely ten minutes to recover her sense of rapport. She didn't let herself think about how long it might take to recover what she had lost with Chris, or if she even could. She lounged in the passenger seat, pushing her palm into the wall of air outside the open window, listening to Chris and Elsie shout stories at each other. Driving with Chris was like flying with him, Lorelei observed. You got the feeling that the world had been created for explorers. You could and *would* go anywhere, and life was a treasure trove of possibility—even in an old wreck of a car. No wonder Chris couldn't be pinned down: he had vagabond blood and gypsy bones.

The woodsy tangle around them changed to half-tamed orchard bounded by old tumbledown stone walls. The sky was an intense and fragile blue, Chris's "severe clear." He turned the car onto a dirt road that led them, jouncing and skidding, up to a hollow in the hillside. A huge old barn rested there in a nest of burnt-orange trees. Half a dozen cars sat around it, and people in plaid jackets and woolly sweaters wandered to and fro.

"I know this isn't the most penetrating observation of my career," Lorelei remarked. "But this place looks like just an old barn."

"Clever disguise, huh?" Chris replied, poker-faced. "It's a cider mill." He shooed the three of them out of the car, and they spent the next half hour examining the goods in the mill. There were jams and honeys, freshly pressed cider and bushels of just-picked apples with the leaves still fluttering from their stems. Elsie bought half a bushel of McIntoshes for the office. Chris got them all cider and doughnuts hot from the oil, and they sat outside at a picnic table stuffing themselves. No one talked a word of business.

When Chris brought them back, the afternoon shadows were long, the sun a flare of fire over the crests of the western hills. Lorelei had missed a dozen important phone calls, but she didn't care. The satisfaction and pleasure in Chris's face as he dropped the car keys into her palm was worth a hundred missed calls. Perhaps the drive had taken them back in time, she thought hopefully—back to the days of their old harmony. She heard Elsie echo a similar sentiment. Her crow's voice carried from the driveway where she had stayed to talk to Chris. "Now that was more like the Chris *I* know. Are you back with us again?"

Lorelei glanced out in time to see Chris bend down and kiss Elsie on the cheek. She hoped that was his way of saying yes.

Chapter Eight

Ah, you're happy, I'm happy—ain't life grand?" Rose was paying one of her state visits to the Teeterbrouck headquarters. Her gleaming Mercedes was parked regally on Chris's lawn. She sparkled like a true star; Pioneer had started sending her out on personal appearances to promote the movie, and she was as happy as a kitten in a warm lap.

"It's a crying shame what power men have over our moods."

Lorelei's head jerked up. She bit back the testy comment that sprang to her lips. "Pray tell, who is this man who has such power over yours? Still the same one you moved to New York for?"

Rosie smiled mysteriously. "Yes. I don't want to jinx it, but I've been making some progress. You just have to learn to present the right image, it seems. He couldn't quite warm up to Rosie the rocker, but Rosie the actress and woman-about-town is getting his attention. Which brings us to how you're doing with your gorgeous playboy. I've noticed you've changed *your* image, and I just wanted to tell you how I approve.''

''I did *not* change my image to get attention... from *anyone*!''

''No? Well, I saw your Apollo out in the yard when I first drove in, and he was all sunshine. You two must have finally reached *some* kind of an understanding or he wouldn't look so happy.''

''My relationship with my employer is just as it should be. Don't go jinxing *me*. God, you're as bad as Sylvia.''

Her sister tossed off the criticism with a flick of her fluffy red mane. ''I'm just eager to see my darling sister enjoying life as much as I am. Isn't there some kind of proverb about that?''

''The one I've found is 'misery loves company.' Just let me do my job, sis. We've got three weeks to go, and if you want your movie career—*your* career, remember—to get launched right, you gotta give me a little room to work. Okay?''

The last thing Lorelei wanted to do was discuss Chris. Since the trip to the cider mill, he had been as sweet as sugar; the man she had first met and liked so well had returned with no explanation, as if from a secret mission. Lorelei chose not to question her good fortune.

The project entered its final stages, and Lorelei's last-minute experts congregated in force: the professional party-throwers, publicity assistants and photographers, the television consultants, security-company representatives, the sound engineers who were to record the whole premiere for release as an album...the list went on and on. Many of them made the trip to Teeterbrouck under protest and then stayed out of choice. Hardened professionals with schedules to keep could sometimes be found playing in the piles of leaves around the house. The equable Chris smiled through it all.

''You've got a good bunch of people working for you, Lorelei,'' he observed one day. They had found a rare moment of privacy together in the kitchen, and he was boiling water for tea to break their steady diet of coffee.

Lorelei leaned her elbows on the cool oak slab of the table and watched him with great pleasure. As the weather had chilled, he had abandoned his sexy tank tops and cutaway T-shirts for sweaters of red and black and woodsy greens. She missed the sight of his muscular arms, as brown as melted caramel. But then again, his tan had faded. He hadn't been able to trek off to the tropics on an Odin mission in weeks. She wondered if he missed the trips. Now he returned from the airport with his cheeks nipped pink by the cold. The blondest streaks of his hair were giving way to its natural deep toffee color, but the sky-blue light still glittered in his eyes.

He needed a sky-blue sweater, she decided, her mind wandering.

Chris sat a mug of tea in front of her and said, "Don't you think?"

"Huh?"

"Your crew—they're very good."

"Oh...yes, they are." She had to stop daydreaming about the way she'd like to dress him! "I've worked with nearly all of them before, under Gil. Every time I met someone good, I made sure to keep him in my address file. I guess bringing the file with me when I left was sort of unethical. Gil will probably accuse me of stealing it, too."

"Too?"

She jumped. The remark had slipped out unplanned. "Sylvia! He says I stole Sylvia—and of course I did."

"She wasn't his slave, officially. Is Gil doing some show right now that he needs the people you've got working for you?"

"Yes, as a matter of fact. He's doing some battle-of-the-bands for a cable rock station. I suppose he's livid that I've tied up all the best lighting and sound people." The man had called her two more times just to harass her. She told herself that his lawsuit was empty talk until she saw an official piece of paper—a subpoena or whatever it was called.

Chris went on, reassuring her. She had to remind herself that he could not know what her special problem was. "The fact that they're working for *you* rather than him has nothing to do with what you're paying them; I know, because I've approved your budget." He gave her a sparkling smile that drove off the dark thoughts of Gil. "So they're obviously working for the *boss* they like. The atmosphere around here is sort of like an Odin mission."

"You mean it feels like we're stranded out in the jungles of Guatemala?"

"Ha! No, not exactly. It's the camaraderie—very nourishing to the soul."

"I was wondering if you missed being on the missions yourself these last weeks."

He shrugged a denial. "Nah, I'm just a fifth wheel on those things, anyway. Once I make the initial arrangements I'm no real use to anybody. I can't tell a detached retina from color blindness. Oh, I admit I can take a mean blood pressure, but all in all the medical people just tolerate me."

"Their loss is my gain." He raised his eyebrow, and Lorelei skittishly wondered if she had been too familiar. "Because *I've* got work for you," she explained. "We've gotten all kind of last-minute offers of help. I'll call it help, anyway. Things like camera companies offering use of their equipment at the premiere if we'll let them pass out fliers, that kind of thing."

He groaned. "A couple of months ago I couldn't pick up a pen at someone's desk without getting frisked for it on the way out. Now everyone's generous. So this is what it means to be a cause célèbre?"

"Yeah, you were right to be wary of it. But there *is* a difference between the celebrity *I've* achieved for you and what *Gil* would have gotten."

"Oh, is there?" He pretended to be skeptical.

"Yeah, with me you can *refuse* all the tacky ad offers. With him you couldn't."

"I'm about to put that to test, my dear. Let's look at what you've got."

Lorelei hurried to get her file from the office and rushed back, afraid someone else would swoop down on Chris in her absence. She got back too late; he stood by the counter helping someone with the medical terminology in a piece of copy. Lorelei sat down and played with her cold tea bag. No sooner had Chris broken free and turned to her than Sylvia flew in and demanded that Lorelei look over someone's press credentials. At the end of half an hour, none of the letters in Lorelei's file had been touched.

"This must be what it's like to rule a country," Chris muttered. "Good thing I never had any political ambitions."

"Just not power hungry enough, huh?"

"Guess not. Terrible weakness, I know, but what can I do?" He grimaced horribly as another intruder poked his head in, saw his expression and made a rapid retreat. "Lorelei, we've got to get out of here."

"To where?"

"I can't tell you. I don't want anybody to hear and follow us. You've just got to trust me."

"Lead on," she said readily.

Chris turned the trip to the car into a routine from a spy movie: he peered around corners, made mad dashes across stretches of open floor and skulked dramatically in shadows. The procedure left Lorelei weak with laughter. She had never thought of him as such a comedian.

"I really should tell Sylvia where I can be reached," she protested as Chris drove toward the road.

"You *can't* be reached—that's the whole point of this exercise. But I *suppose* you can call in for messages. Yeah, I'll let you do that. Just don't give away our location. We may need it again."

Their "location" proved to be the airport. Maggie made a great fuss over them, complaining that she hadn't seen them in months. Her fuss reminded Lorelei of the peaceful days she had spent camped out in the canteen, listening to Maggie man the Unicom and waiting for the smooth hum of the incoming Duchess. Those had been good days, she thought. She was lucky to be getting another one. In fact, it was a better one. This time she had Chris right there with her.

They sat at one of the chipped tables with a pot of Maggie's pitch-black coffee and worked, happily surrounded by photographs of Maggie's favorite aviators. Once in a while the throaty sound of an airplane ruffled the quiet like a light breeze rippling the surface of a pond. Occasionally an engine sputtered on the ground near the hangars and voices were raised in discussion. No matter how intent Chris seemed to be upon a task, he always cocked his head to listen. "Sounds like Johnson's little ultralight," he would say, or "Jim got the Pitts working again." Lorelei realized that the sound of every airplane was as particular to him as the voice of a friend.

These small interruptions were friendly notes in the peaceful afternoon. Lorelei watched Maggie in the office making entries in her big old logbook and thought, this wouldn't be a bad life. Perhaps once the premiere was over she should come up once in a while, have a piece of Maggie's pie and watch the airplanes.... Then she looked at Chris as he bent over a query letter—the long, straight line of his nose, the dark, narrow triangles of his lowered eyes, and she knew that *he* was what made it so wonderful. Without him, or the promise of his being there, Teeterbrouck's airfield would be a lonely place for her.

"Listen to this," Chris complained in an irate voice. "These people actually want to film a mouthwash commercial on one of our jets."

Lorelei rallied from her daydream. "But it's a very strong *antiseptic* mouthwash. Maybe we could show our surgeons sterilizing their equipment in it."

Chris stared at her, momentarily stumped by her seriousness. Then he rolled his eyes, and she laughed. "File in an appropriate manner," he ordered. "Next victim."

"Next victim?" The unexpected sound of a male voice grabbed their attention. Lorelei recognized the tall, stocky man as one of the airplane hobbyists who made Maggie's field his second home. All of them knew Chris and treated him as a favorite son. This one tipped his beaked cap to Lorelei and plunked himself down on the table.

Maggie's voice came skirling out of the office. "Get your butt off that table, Calvin Reyes! It's unappetizing!"

The man hopped off and winked elaborately at Chris and Lorelei.

"Lorelei," Chris said, "this is Cal Reyes. Cal—Lorelei Chant."

"How d'ya do? You've put in some hours at this table. I remember seeing you here." Cal reached out a bear paw of a hand and shook hers. "What's all this, Chris? I thought at first you might be conducting ground school for the young lady, but I guess not."

"Nope, it's honest work. Us young folks have to keep paying into social security so you old fakers can play all day."

"Aw, you're breaking my heart, Chrissie."

Lorelei had never heard anyone call Chris "Chrissie." He didn't seem to mind—perhaps, she thought, his pilot buddies could get away with more than others could.

"How's that antique of yours, Cal? You give up and junk it yet?"

"Nah, she's all fixed up." He launched into a detailed technical report on exactly how he had fixed up his old aircraft.

Though Lorelei tried to follow, the aviation jargon lost her. The next thing she understood clearly was Cal's suggestion that they come out and admire his handiwork. Chris agreed in an instant. "Come on, Lorelei. This is a great airplane."

"You go ahead, I'll keep on with the work."

"And how are you going to do that without me? You'll enjoy this, I promise."

"Is this another one of your timid little attempts to prove you're not a slave driver like Gil?"

"I hadn't thought of it like that—but yeah, I guess it is." He let her set her coffee mug on a pile of loose papers, then took her hand and firmly pulled her out of the canteen.

Cal's plane was the bright orange thing she had seen in pieces all summer long. During the weeks she had spent avoiding Teeterbrouck, he had actually finished fiddling and put the pieces together. It was an open-cockpit biplane with a rugged look to it. Lorelei obediently looked at everything the proud owner pointed out and tried to "ooh" and "ah" at appropriate moments. Her real pleasure came from watching Chris. Airplane buff that he was, he understood why the plane was so great. He circled the craft with Cal, asking all the right questions. Lorelei thought what a boon it must be for him to have such a consuming passion. It took his mind off Odin from time to time.

When Cal walked away for a moment, she murmured cautiously to Chris, "Now that he's gone, will you tell me *why* this airplane is so special?"

"It's a 1944 Stearman—an old U.S. mail plane, a very historic beast. Cal's put in a really powerful engine so he can use it for aerobatics."

"You mean loop-the-loops and that kind of thing?"

"Yep. He used to fly in a weekend air show farther upstate. He can do hammerheads and barrel rolls in his sleep."

"Sounds like the safest way to do them." Cal returned and Lorelei shut up.

"You two want to take her for a spin?"

A spin? From what Chris had said about the airplane, Lorelei knew Cal probably meant a literal spin, but she failed to decline in time.

"Yet bet!" Chris grinned. "How about it, Lorelei? You trust my flying yet?"

"I trust *it* fine..." She almost said it was her stomach she didn't trust, but he looked so happy, so hopeful of having her share his enthusiasm, that she stoically forbore. "Okay, but no hammerheads, all right? I don't like them as sharks in the water, and I'm sure I won't like them as whatever they are in the air."

"No hammerheads," he promised. "Might do a couple inverted loops though."

Chris limited himself to a few very mild maneuvers, and he constantly glanced over his shoulder to see how Lorelei was holding up. To her own surprise, she weathered the noisy, windy, disorienting flight in the open cockpit much better than she ever had carnival rides—due, she was sure, to her confidence in the pilot.

"You've got a good head for aerobatics," he declared after they landed.

"Of course. Stunt flying is very similar to rock and roll."

"I'll have to think about that for a while," he said, scratching his head.

Back in the canteen their ebullience faded; the work lay waiting for them."Sort of an anticlimax," Lorelei grumbled.

Before they could start, Maggie appeared. "It's dinnertime. You two either have to clean up and leave or clean up and eat with the family."

Lorelei checked her watch in alarm. "My God, it *is* that late. Chris, we've got to go back! I've left Sylvia on her own with all those people."

"I guess we should. Can't keep the world at bay forever—not even flying."

She studied him as they packed up and headed for the car. Was that why he flew? To keep the world at bay? He had certainly chosen an intrusive world to keep out. Odin managed to involve every aspect of one's life. Why hadn't he stayed down in Argentina herding cattle or whatever he had been doing when John Ward had met him? Lorelei knew nothing about such a job, but she strongly suspected that, as demanding as it might be in the air, it was over once you landed. With Odin, Chris's worries *multiplied* once he landed.

"Wait a minute." She snapped out of her musings. "This isn't the way home."

"Home, huh? You really take your work to heart, don't you?"

She blushed and struggled to reply evenly. "Don't try to distract me. This still isn't the way back."

"We have an errand in town."

We? she wondered.

The errand turned out to be buying pizzas. After ordering, she and Chris roamed around Teeterbrouck in the gathering dusk, talking airplanes and holding on to the happy mood of the flight. They were still cheerful when they collected the pizzas and drove back to the office.

Elsie had gone home, as had most of the crowd. But Sylvia and a couple of others remained. Chris presided over dinner, seeming to enjoy being the host for a change rather than the boss.

As Lorelei drove Sylvia home to Nyack that evening, enjoying her warm memories of the day, Sylvia babbled. "Sorry I didn't get all these catering arrangements done for you, Lorelei."

"What? Oh, no problem—they can wait."

"They can? This isn't the Lorelei I know and love. What did your gorgeous superboss do this afternoon to get you so mellowed out?"

Lorelei unmellowed instantly. "Nobody needs to *do* anything to me. Am I really such a tyrant?"

Sylvia ignored the question. "Did *you* get a lot of work done . . . wherever it was you went?"

"If you must know, *yes*, we did get a lot done." Although perhaps not as much as we *could* have, she reminded herself.

"Um-hum . . ."

Sylvia's "um-hum" had a sly curl to it. Lorelei tried to read the girl's face in the darkness and thought she saw a smug look of satisfaction. "I know I'll be sorry I asked, but what did *that* mean?"

"Just that it's nice seeing you in a good mood, both of you. Would you like to hear my theory?"

"No."

"I think that if you two had met socially you'd be stuck on each other like a couple of Gummi Bears."

"Sylvia! That's disgusting!" She laughed in spite of herself.

"Well, okay, you're too dignified, maybe you're not the Gummi Bear type. But *Chris* is a sweetie. Just you try and deny it—buying pizzas for all these strangers we've dumped on him. You give him half a chance and—"

"I don't want to hear any more about this."

"You two just need more time together in situations that don't make you tense. Something less business-y, more social."

"Not much chance of that," Lorelei said wistfully. "From now until the premiere it's one long superhighway of tension." She realized too late that Sylvia would interpret this in the worst possible way—as an admission that she *wanted* time alone with Chris. "If you've still got time and energy enough to play soap opera with my alleged love life, I'd be very glad to give you more work, Syl."

" 'Alleged love life.' You see, that has such a sad sound

to it. You ought to get an award for celibacy."

"I *ought* to get a new assistant."

Sylvia shut up for a couple of days after that, but her air of secretiveness, the lowered voice she used on the telephone and her increased zest for life set Lorelei on edge. More suspicious still, Rosie called at least once a day—never for Lorelei, always for Sylvia. Lorelei knew all was not as it should have been.

Chris, however, was just as he should have been—sweet, gallant and so handsome it hurt her to look at him. The various females who had business at the house swooned over him even more than usual. Lorelei considered trying to interest Sylvia in meddling with their love lives instead, but when she realized that Chris would still be part of her manipulations, she dropped the idea.

One morning Rosie broke her pattern and called for Lorelei. "Howdy, little sister."

"Well, this is a surprise. I thought I had finally weaned you off me and on to Sylvia."

"Do I hear a note of pique in your voice?"

"Sorry, just my suspicious mind grinding away again. I can't help but worry when people like you and Sylvia get chummy."

"Oops, you've found us out. Sylvia's breaking off to start her own producing career, and she's luring me away as a client . . . Lorelei? Are you there?"

"Bad joke, Rosie."

"I'm sorry, honey. No one ever accused me of good judgment."

"Let's find another subject. Are you still enjoying your life as a professional talk-show guest? It's going to get pretty full the final week before the premiere."

"Honey, I'm getting to where I want my own. 'The Rose Champlain Show,' or 'Talk with Rosie' or something like that. Maybe you can suggest it to your TV buddies. I've been suggesting it to Owen until he's sick of me."

A certain affectionate note seemed to ring in the way Rosie said the name of the movie's producer. Lorelei proceeded carefully. "Does he have any *other* suggestions for your career?"

"Oh, yes," Rosie warbled. "We talk about it all the time. I don't think I'll ever make a move without him again."

"No? Gotten that close, have you?"

Rosie lapsed into a jumpy silence, then giggled quietly. "Guess I should tell you. That 'pending' situation with a man has moved over to the 'active' file."

"Owen Browne, huh?" A perfectly nice man, Lorelei admitted. He had been generous with his help on the project, though she had assumed that was purely because of his interest in the *film*. "You haven't found it . . . awkward working with him and . . . er . . ."

"*And?* Honey, you're so prim you're cute. No, I haven't found it awkward. He never would have looked twice at me a year ago. We would have met and gone our separate ways, me with a broken heart. Thank goodness this movie kept us knocking into each other. He's a wonderful man—the best. But he's still a man. You know—dumb about women."

Lorelei grunted noncommittally. Was there a *true* parallel between her sister's situation and her own, or did she just want there to be? Did she wish that Chris's reticence could be put down to being "dumb about women?" "Well, I hope your persistence was worth it, sis. I like everything I know about Owen so far, but I admit I'm going to look at him a lot more critically next time I see him."

"About that . . . We're really getting down to the wire on this premiere. I think it's time the principals got together and did something—you know, to kick off the stretch run. I feel in need of a symbolic little event."

Lorelei's suspicious brain cranked into action again. In her sister's talk, she detected a whiff of Sylvia. She thought of the secret calls back and forth. Rosie was not *suggesting* a "symbolic event;" one had already been planned. "What 'principals' are you talking about?"

"Oh, me, Owen, John Ward and his wife, you, Chris..."

"Uh-huh." There was nothing intrinsically wrong, professionally wrong, with such a group getting together. Business associates did it all the time and wrote it off on their taxes. Lorelei's desire to steer clear of social events with Chris ran contrary to the rest of the business world. "What exactly did you have in mind?"

"Nothing extravagant, just drinks and dinner—the usual. We'll even make it easy for you and Chris; we can go to that place you told me about months ago, that yacht-club place. Owen and I wouldn't mind getting out of the city for an evening, and the Wards live up there somewhere, don't they?"

"They live in Greenwich, Connecticut. It's not exactly 'up here,' but I guess it's not a bad drive."

"Good. Look, I'll make all the arrangements. You just line Chris up. Or do you want me to do that, too?"

The temptation was formidable, but Lorelei overcame it. "No, I'll talk to him. Pick a time."

"How about tomorrow, sevenish?"

"Okay. I'll call you if he can't make it." Lorelei put down the phone and sat silently at her desk. The neighboring office was noticeably quiet. Elsie was out but Sylvia should have been making *some* kind of noise—unless she was listening. "Wouldn't it be better if you listened on your *phone*, Sylvia?" Lorelei called. "Then you could hear *both* sides of the conversation."

There was another moment of silence before Sylvia answered, not a bit deflated, "Rosie can tell me what she said on her end."

Lorelei presented the dinner plan to Chris as he took apart a navigation radio at the kitchen table. She would have preferred to sit all morning and watch his long, sensitive fingers trim wire and turn tiny little screws, but it was not one of her options.

"I must be dreaming this," he commented. "The Lorelei Chant who has to be kidnapped before she'll take a few hours off is suggesting a frivolous night on the town?"

"Not *suggesting*—I couldn't come up with any good excuse to refuse. It's Owen Browne, after all."

Chris kept his head down, but Lorelei thought she saw the edges of a grin.

"And anyway, it's hardly a night on the town. I mean, this is *Teeterbrouck*, not Atlantic City."

He looked up, pouting as if he had been hurt. "I thought you liked Teeterbrouck."

"Like a brother. Now, are we going?"

"With bells on . . . seeing as it's not your idea."

To Sylvia's quiet horror, Lorelei spent the next day in jeans. The girl had enough sense not to complain out loud, but her relief was clear when at 6:15 Lorelei changed. "What a stunning dress! I don't remember ever seeing it before."

"It's new," Lorelei replied tersely. "But I did *not* buy it especially for tonight, if that's what your sly little brain cells are suggesting."

"The thought never entered my head," Sylvia protested. "You know, that blue-green color is really flattering. You always looked terrific in the bright reds and purples you used to wear, but these more subtle colors lately have been wonderful. You should—"

"Shut up, Sylvia."

Sylvia sniffed and went away. Lorelei couldn't help but glance at herself in the mirror. It was a good outfit—a soft, loosely knit wool dress with a big scoop neck that showed off her creamy skin and her one good piece of jewelry, a pearl necklace. The effect was attractive but still fairly de-

telephones. She was young, cute and stylish, just the way Gilman liked them. By her voice, she was the girl who had so effectively rebuffed him on the phone. Smiling from the doorway, he caught her eyes and sauntered in, beaming charm. She put all her callers on hold.

"Hi, what can I do for you?"

Good, he thought, her tone had been quite inviting. "Good afternoon. And I must say it's gotten considerably better since I came upon your pretty face. I'm—"

"Christian Jansen," she finished for him. "I never forget a voice."

"Is that so?" He grinned, stalling for time. He had planned on claiming to be an old buddy of Gilman's, a thought that sent shudders through him. Now he wouldn't have to. "I'll bet you're worth your weight in gold to Gil. I hope he appreciates you."

"Not nearly enough."

Chris settled himself boldly on the edge of her desk. She didn't complain. "Do you also know why I'm here?"

"I hope it's to tell him how terrific I am, but you didn't know that when you called for the appointment, so I suppose not.... I'm afraid I still can't get you in to see him. He's left for the day, he really has."

"I believe you."

"Are you a friend of his or a business associate?"

"Neither, and I'd honestly like to keep it that way."

"Wise," she allowed.

"But I have information for him...pertaining to a lawsuit he's bringing against one of his former employees."

Her black-lined eyes went round as records. "He's suing a former employee?"

Chris saw that he had ignited something in her—fear or considerable enmity. As usual, all was not love and chocolates between Gilman and his staff. "Yes, he is—unless, of course, he changes his mind after what I have to tell him."

"Can you leave a message with me?"

He bent closer and lowered his voice. "Well, I would, but you know what they do to the bearer of bad tidings. I'd prefer you didn't have to tell him yourself."

She stared at the blinking telephone lights. "So that's what Sylvia's been calling about..." She looked up, frowning. "He's hassling Lorelei, isn't he?"

Chris winced. He hadn't intended to let Lorelei's name come into it. "Do you know her?"

"No, but I know Sylvia and I've heard stories...all in Lorelei's favor, you understand."

He gave her a significant look. "They would have to be. That's the problem. Gilman's afraid of the competition."

"You're a friend of Lorelei's?"

Chris allowed himself to nod. "Sylvia will vouch for me. Do you want the phone number where she can be reached?"

"No, I think this is one intrigue I'd like to stay out of." She gripped the rim of her desk for a moment, as if steeling herself. "You'd better catch Gil quick—he leaves tomorrow for two weeks on the West Coast. But right now he's having dinner at Revolver."

He gave her hand a light but earnest kiss and hopped off the desk. Her last comment caught him at the door. "Hey, don't tell him how you found him, or I might be asking Lorelei if she needs another assistant."

"If so, I'll put in a good word for you," he promised, thinking how little good his word would do anyone with Lorelei.

"The name's Stephanie."

He winked and left. He would not be quite so amiable with Gilman.

Chris spent the forty blocks between Rockefeller Center and Revolver walking off the pleasant mood he had used to charm Stephanie. At Twenty-sixth Street he was assailed by memories of the day he had so grudgingly collected Lorelei and her little store of equipment and trucked them home to Teeterbrouck. Even then, deep down, he had known that

she was not involved in some scurrilous female plot to en-
snare him. She had too much honesty and integrity for that,
neither of which had helped her deal with him.

He pressed on toward Greenwich Village, working up the
proper wrath with which to face Gilman. The restaurant was
as dark and noisy as ever, but the clientele looked less
trendy. Chris wondered why Gilman still used the place. He
was the type who abandoned people and things as soon as
they had passed their peak of stylishness.

The hostess remembered him and willingly pointed out
Gilman's table. Like the restaurant, Gilman seemed to have
slid down a trendy rung or two. Or perhaps it was Chris's
always-low opinion of him that had deteriorated. His ve-
lour sweat jacket was still half-unzipped to display the top
of his hairy gray chest, and his voice still rumbled over those
of his table companions like a runaway truck. He exuded
terminal lack of class. The thought of him getting his foul
hands on Lorelei's life again made Chris go cold with resolve. She had certainly had a bad run of men in her life—
if he and Gilman constituted a run.

Chris gathered himself to make a low-key attack and
hoped he wouldn't do anything that Alan Hatfield couldn't
patch up. Settling out of court was one thing, but settling at
a restaurant in front of a bunch of respectable-looking wit-
nesses bordered on the uncivilized. Chris reminded himself
that he was hardly civilized; he had already proved that. He
strolled forward, catching the eyes of the two couples at the
table but coming up behind Gilman. There was an empty
chair next to him. With exaggerated nonchalance, Chris
pushed it out of the way and stood at the man's side.

"Evening, folks. Sorry to barge in on you, but Mr. Gilman and I have about five minutes of business to take care
of before he runs off tomorrow."

Gilman flared. "Who the hell..." Then he squinted.
"*Jansen.*"

"Good, you remember me." Chris swung himself into the empty chair. "I'd hate to think you go around suing people you don't remember."

"The suit is against that bit—Lorelei. It's none of *your* business."

"On the contrary, it's my business in a couple of very important ways. Give it some thought."

Gilman obviously did just that, and his marble-hard eyes shifted nervously.

Chris addressed the whole table with his next remark; they were interested. "Now, Gil, not to brag, but Odin is a hot ticket these days—everybody's favorite cause. How's it going to look for you if it comes out that you're trying to sabotage us just to get even with some little girl who used to work for you? Especially if you lose the lawsuit, which my lawyers assure me you will."

"You're way out of line here, Jansen." The fidgety little man eyed his companions uneasily. "This is between me and that little ingrate who used inside information—among *other* things—to steal my client."

"Get a grip, Gilman. *I'm* the client you say she stole. Do I look stolen?" He appealed comically to the two couples. All four people looked fascinated, and no one seemed to have much sympathy for Gilman. "Now, Gil, I know you're just trying to throw the premiere of *The Veldt* into confusion. You have no real intention of letting this suit get to court, and we've already established that it would be bad press for you if it got into the news. But I tell you honestly, I may not be able to keep it quiet much longer. I've got reporters on me all the time. Maybe you should give Lorelei one last call, a nice one. If not—" he sighed "—you'll be hearing from my attorney Alan Hatfield—of Hatfield, Tanner and Lowe."

Chris stood and made polite goodbyes to the mute quintet. The owner of the seat he had usurped stood to one side, having returned. She looked mystified, but the others, excluding Gilman, looked amused.

Chris paused outside the restaurant, letting the cold revive him. The confrontation had been exhausting. He had very little practice threatening people and making scenes, and he hoped he never got any more. This ordeal had been for Lorelei—small recompense for the harm he had done her, but *something*. Now if only it worked.

Chapter Ten

If Chris had expected to hear anything definite from Gilman or Hatfield or *anyone* assuring him that the lawsuit had been dropped, he was disappointed. The days went by without a sign that he'd had any effect. His house continued to be overrun by people working on the final preparations for the premiere, but none of them was Lorelei. He didn't see her until two days before the event, when she called a major powwow for everyone involved. Even the "useless execs," as Sylvia termed them, were "strongly urged to attend." Chris took the urging seriously.

He showed up at midday in front of the Metropolitan Plaza in Manhattan's theater district. The gray, blustery day reminded him poignantly of the day he had met Lorelei in front of the Teeterbrouck Cinema. She had been wearing some shocking yellow outfit, one of her rock and roll costumes. She had been bright and buoyant with enthusiasm, and edgy that he would not respond in kind.

But Lorelei didn't meet him this time. Sylvia did, and she stuck a hot-pink pass on his lapel to get him past the security guards. The lobby of the grand old theater bustled with scores of people he didn't know and some he remembered from the house, all hurrying to get into the auditorium.

"Who are all these people?" he asked in amazement.

"I guess they're technically your employees, Chris. Yours and Pioneer's. They're the ushers, the stagehands, the projectionists and sound men..." She rattled off half a dozen more categories as she showed him into the auditorium and sat him with some people from the film company. She pressed a sheet of paper into his hands. "You'll get the schedule for the dress rehearsal and the actual show later," she said. Then she dashed down the aisle toward the stage.

Chris looked at the paper. It was a map of the theater and a schedule of that day's events. The afternoon had been broken into separate meetings for each specialized worker. His name had been written at the top in red, and there were red asterisks placed beside the meetings someone—Lorelei?—thought he should attend: General Introduction, Press/Media and Performers. Performers, he mused. He was scheduled to be introduced onstage briefly. That made him a performer?

The young executive next to him leaned over with a grin and tapped his own sheet of paper. "Feels like assembly on the first day of school, doesn't it?"

Chris agreed vaguely.

"Ah, here comes teacher."

Chris's gaze shot to the stage. A slim figure in a Day-Glo-orange dress, the color of which made her look like a highway signal flag, had stepped up to the podium. Her silvery-blond hair was scraped back into a straight braid, and she held herself with great precision. Chris detected no trace of the strain she must be feeling. She really was good at this, he thought, feeling a sense of pride he probably had no right to.

"Okay, gang," she said into the mike. "We've only got ninety minutes to go over a lot of material, so don't fall asleep on me or neck with your date or go out for popcorn, okay?"

The crowd laughed, and the meeting got off to a cheerful start.

Ninety minutes later on the dot, it ended with a break for lunch. Chris had a brand-new appreciation of the complex event about to transpire, every detail of which had been conceived, planned and run by one twenty-five-year-old girl. He marveled at it all through lunch, which he ate with the visiting president of Max Tech. Then he obediently reported back to the theater for his "Press/Media" meeting.

This proved to be a smaller venture, held in one of the theater's auxiliary rooms. Chris found himself with the people who would clear press credentials and manage the invited reporters. All the principals of Odin and Pioneer had been included, since they would be talking to press people as well. John Ward hailed him from across the room, and Chris joined him.

Lorelei and Sylvia appeared with stacks of printed material to hand out—the press kits, all the various brochures that would be available at the premiere, and a very long list of cleared media people. Lorelei surveyed her little audience, and before she tore them away, her eyes locked with Chris's. Then she began her talk. She had fascinating information for them: tips on how to field awkward questions, instructions on when and where the performers could be collared for interviews and which people were the experts in which fields. Chris's mind betrayed him with its tendency to drift into private fantasies despite the lively talk, but his attention snapped back abruptly when Lorelei introduced him and John as the experts on Odin. That done, she ignored him again, and he slipped back into reverie.

He had two more days of her company, two more days that she would still be bound to Odin. She had become such a part of his life; in some stubborn part of his mind he had assumed she always would be. Maybe it was better that she wouldn't, he told himself. He needed to make a clean break so he could get his wits under control again. Just looking at her today had brought him pain. She had never looked more beautiful. She always seemed most gloriously herself, and thus more attractive, when she was hard at work. Getting over her would be as easy as getting over breathing.

At the end of the session, Ward tied Chris up in seemingly endless chatter. Lorelei had left before he could break free. He glared around at the cold concrete walls of the theater's backstage area. The desire to say something to her— even a few bland pleasantries—heated up in him like a fever. He checked the printed schedule, truly feeling like a schoolboy. The next session Lorelei was scheduled to hold did not meet for half an hour yet, and she could have gone anywhere. On a whim, he searched his map for the command post and went to it.

She was there, sitting on a musty green couch, enjoying an uncharacteristic moment of peace.

"Busy?" he asked quietly. He felt oddly shy about breaking in on her.

"No. Have a seat."

He resisted the urge to take one next to her on the couch and forced himself to make do with an armchair. Her shoeless, stockinged feet were propped up on a scratched coffee table. They looked as if they needed a massage and the caress of soft slippers. When she noticed where his attention had gone, she tucked her legs up under her and smoothed her dress over her knees. Embarrassed, Chris let his eyes sweep the room. "Looks familiar, doesn't it? I mean, of *course* it looks familiar to you, but it even does to me—another backstage junk pile."

"You're becoming a veteran."

"Does Giants Stadium count on my résumé?"

"Anything that calls upon you to save someone from allergic shock counts for *something*." A soft look came into her face, Chris could feel his heart leap into his throat.

"Hope that doesn't happen again."

"Well..." She shrugged. "It would be okay if you were around to take care of it."

"Do you *want* me around?" The amount of longing in his voice scared him. He hurried on. "Is there anything I can do between now and the premiere?"

She answered in her professional voice, staring at a stain on the coffee table. "No, I'd just like you to show up to be introduced to the audience onstage and for the photos and interviews with the VIPs backstage. You're good at all that stuff; you make a good impression."

He leaned forward and found himself saying softly, "With everyone but you. Lorelei, I—"

She bolted to her feet and scrambled for the door. Chris got to her just before she managed to open it. He leaned his shoulder firmly against the wood and caught hold of her hands. They were trembling violently, and she wouldn't look at him. "Lorelei, what can I say—"

"I really have to get out there, Chris. I have a show to run."

He released her and slumped against the wall. "I know. I suppose you really don't need me mucking up your concentration right now."

"No, not really."

He had no right to be annoyed with her, but he felt a sharp flare of impatience. She had always been his sweet Lorelei, his forgiving Lorelei. He needed her sweetness and forgiveness right now. Where were they? His reason reminded him that she had already given him much more than he deserved. He moved aside in resignation and held the door open for her. She stepped quickly to the threshold, hesitated and let her jade-green eyes flick upward to his. Her words came out low and hurried. "Thank you for taking care of Gil for me. I meant to say that before."

Then she was gone.

On the morning of the premiere, Lorelei rose hours before the sun. She had not really slept in several days, relying instead on troubled catnaps. Between leaving Gil and starting with Odin she had run several events, but none had led her to expect the nerve-racking nature of running Odin's. Tension was to be expected, but always before it had been the tension of eagerness and energy, not the debilitating terror that sometimes caught hold of her now. As she showered and dressed in the outfit she had chosen to make her easily visible backstage, black trousers and a blaring lime-green sweater, she identified the source of her tension—Chris. But knowing didn't help her relax one bit.

She got to the theater early in order to enjoy its temporary peacefulness. The morning commuters on their way to work hurried past her with barely a look, too preoccupied to notice the signs that something momentous was soon to take place in the old art-deco theater. Had they looked up, they might have noticed the new gold-and-black marquee that read Exclusive Engagement—Max Weiman's *THE VELDT* Starring Rosie Champlain—Madrid Film Festival's Best Picture. They might have wondered at the fluttering banners announcing American Premiere Tonight. Rosie had already photographed the whole scene from every angle.

The theater's manager and the foreman of the teamsters met Lorelei at the loading dock in the alley. Since the theater had once been used for live shows, it had the necessary ramps and backstage rooms for a big production, but the trucks found it a tight squeeze in the alley.

"Good morning, Miss Chant," the foreman started pleasantly. "Hope you've had your morning coffee already."

"Why? What's wrong?"

"Nothing major, the truck lift broke down. We're fixing it, but unloading's backed up a bit."

Her first problem—not a huge one, just big enough to kick start her mind. She pulled out her clipboard to see how far behind schedule they were.

By nine, Sylvia and Lorelei's other lieutenants had arrived. They conferred together and took over their separate duties. Everyone looked bright and eager and full of enviable confidence. The morning passed quickly, a stream of activity occasionally churned by small problems. Lorelei smoothed them out or found ways to go around. By the eleven o'clock break, several of the principal "useless execs" had stopped by to get in the way: Owen Browne, John Ward, and Max Weiman himself. Chris was conspicuously absent. Lorelei longed to ask Ward where his baffling friend was hiding, but could not make the words leave her lips.

Sylvia was the one who asked, reading Lorelei's mind in a disturbingly astute way. "Hey, Dr. Ward, us plebes have been up since the crack of doom slaving away. Where's our fearless leader, Chris? Getting the beauty sleep he hardly needs?"

"Up in Rochester. He had to go up yesterday to soothe the nerves of that pharmaceutical company—the people who gave us that great big check. Some magazine ran an editorial about the black marketeering of drugs given as foreign aid, and now the directors of the company are all flustered. Chris will calm them down. He's a good tranquilizer."

Like heck, Lorelei thought to herself. Then she busily shuffled checklists to hide her reaction. Chris had a rather different effect on *her*.

Concern made Sylvia breathless. "He's not going to miss the premiere, is he?"

"No," Ward reassured her. "He should have left there by now, in fact. He'll be back at Teeterbrouck field by mid-afternoon. Plenty of time to put on the old tux and get down here."

Lorelei did calculations in her head. He'd have to take care of his airplane, drive home, shower and change, drive into the city.... With any luck, she wouldn't have to see him until the actual start of the show. Until then she'd have plenty to keep her from thinking about him.

That was the theory, anyway. The reality was that one part of her mind seemed especially designed to dwell on him no matter how she occupied the rest. Midafternoon came—the probable time of his landing. Lorelei felt the small knot of tension in her stomach clench harder as if she had unconsciously been keeping track, waiting for him to be safe on the ground again. Strange, she thought, his flying had never bothered her before.

The hours passed and the knot tightened. She thought fretfully that *someone* should have heard from him, if not her then John Ward—and Ward would have sought her out with any news. A simple call to his house would have settled her mind, but she shied away from picking up the phone. She remembered how abruptly she had treated Chris two days before when he had come to see her. A fool could have seen that he was trying to apologize, but she had cut him off, turned her back on him. Her sudden concern now would seem a bit false. No, she'd force herself to be patient. He'd show up in his own good time.

At six o'clock she hid herself in the dark booth of a nearby restaurant. Her brain had started to spin like a tire on the ice. Sound checks, lighting checks, security checks! The fire marshal had shown up looking grim and insisted on going over the emergency procedures with her one more time. Part of Rosie's costume—her pith helmet—had gone astray, and a TV crew had arrived forty-five minutes past their assigned time, still expecting to film their spot. Lorelei desperately needed a half hour of peace.

So she sat in her dim booth with her eyes closed and a cold plate of lasagne in front of her. The hum of conversation from the unseen people at other booths and tables soothed her. They seemed a happy lot, carefree, with their day's work behind them and the evening ahead reserved for fun, or so she imagined. She started to notice particular conversations and became aware of the number of couples around her. Some had the easy intimacy of people who knew each other well, like John and Irene Ward. Some were silly and excited, like Rosie and her executive beau. Hearing them overturned all the progress Lorelei had made on relaxing. She suddenly felt cut off from the human race. Everyone in the world seemed to be finding another soul to keep him or her company, even if for only one night. *She* was running an extravaganza, and the man she loved was slipping on a tuxedo, preparing to walk into her life and out of it one last time. The man she loved... The booth seemed to close in oppressively. She abandoned her lasagne and fled back to the Metropolitan.

When she saw the crowd pressing against the barricades in front of the theater, the fact finally came home to her that she had done it—she had created Odin's event. From this night forward, the world would know the foundation's name. No more would it be an unsung little pocket of heroism, no more would Chris have to beg, cajole and sweat out every dollar of its budget. Until the public forgot again, anyway.

Glowing with an unfamiliar feeling of pride, Lorelei showed her pass to the policeman and squeezed through the barricades. Camera bulbs flashed as people took her photo and tried to figure out who she was. That they never would didn't bother her. No public recognition would surpass the satisfaction she felt at just having done the work.

Inside the lobby, technicians were clearing away cables and equipment from the delayed TV segment. Lorelei spied her sister talking to reporters in the middle of the room. Owen flanked her, trying without much luck to look staunch and unflappable. He *should* have been coaxing Rosie back to her dressing room. Lorelei strode forward to take charge.

"I see you got your pith helmet."

Rosie beamed. "And it's even the right size. That nice young redheaded boy of yours bought it downtown. I remember him from somewhere, don't I?"

"You may very well—he was Gil's gofer when I left." She propelled Rosie out of the lobby as they talked, trailing Owen.

"Another employee theft? Lorelei, you *cad*." Rosie grinned wickedly. "I wonder if we'll see your old fire-breather here tonight."

"Gil? Heavens, Rosie, I didn't *invite* him. That would have been too much like rubbing it in."

"But he's got a lot of friends, he could get in if he wanted to. If he's curious enough...."

"I think he'll stay clear...." She hesitated. "He called one last time and made a speech about me hiding behind Chris and his shysters. Evidently Chris scared him off."

"I *thought* it'd be a good idea for Chris to know," Rosie declared smugly. They had reached her small dressing room. Huge bouquets of flowers covered most of the banged-up furniture.

"You opening up a florist shop or something?" Lorelei joked, ignoring the previous comment. "I thought you had finally gotten serious about your movie career."

Rosie sank luxuriously into the couch and sniffed at a mass of anemones. "Aren't they lovely? These are from your golden boy, Chris. Where is he, anyway? I thought surely he'd drop by and say hello before now. I want a *lot* of pictures taken of me draped over his totally stunning arm—for the gossip columnists." She winked at Owen.

A jab of unease stuck Lorelei, but she didn't let it show. "I'll check on him for you, Sis. He probably got snared by someone with a problem. You know how they zero in on him."

"Yeah, the good Christian. He's a soft touch for *almost* anybody."

Lorelei didn't care to hear what Rosie meant by *almost* anybody. She hoisted her clipboard and escaped to the corridor. Half a dozen people immediately swooped down upon her with questions. As she answered each, her eyes scanned the crowd for sight of one particular golden head. She found the steely-gray one that belonged to John Ward. He looked troubled. Lorelei broke away and hurried over to him.

"John, what's the problem? And where's your fly-boy partner?"

"*That's* the problem—I don't know. Chris said he'd meet me almost an hour ago but there's no sign of him. He's not the type who'd be late just to make an entrance, you know. If he says he'll meet you at a certain time, he will."

"Well, maybe he didn't take off on time, maybe he had to fix a mechanical problem or wait out a storm or something. What's the weather like between here and Rochester?" Lorelei tried to sound unconcerned and believe her own suggestions—Chris must have been grounded by a small glitch. He'd miss the premiere, but he wouldn't be a pile of charred wreckage on some upstate meadow.

"The weather was clear when I talked with him this morning. There's a little overcast sitting above Sullivan and Orange counties, but he said he'd be flying well over that."

"There must be some way to check on him!" Lorelei cried. She caught the edge of desperation in her voice and tried to dull it. "I mean, I don't need him to be introduced onstage so much, but he really should be here to answer questions. Rosie's going to be swamped by press, and she doesn't know *everything*."

Ward frowned at her as if her speech had struck him wrong. Of course it had, she reasoned. Ward was worried about Chris as a friend, not as a member of the cast, and he had every right to expect her to feel that way, too. "I'm just on my way to make a few phone calls," he answered gruffly. "I'll let you know as soon as I learn anything."

"Thank you, I appreciate that." As Ward turned his back on her and hurried away, Lorelei's nonchalance crumbled. Something had happened to Chris.

The ground below the Duchess was a patchwork of gold and brown and orange; it looked like an Early American quilt. The sky ahead was hazy, not the rarified blue that Chris preferred, and puffy clouds drifted toward him, but he had satisfied himself with the weather report—no fronts were due to blow in until nightfall. By that time he'd be safely on the ground at the Metropolitan Plaza. As safe as he could be, at least, on his last night with Lorelei.

Trimming the airplane after it bounced through a pocket of turbulence, he considered what a mess he had made of things. He managed to sweet-talk, charm and out-argue the most prickly foreign officials; he calmed irate, exhausted doctors; cheered nurses through their bleakest despair. Yet all his tact had been useless with Lorelei. Or rather, it had been unused. He had certainly been right that she would wrench his life off its hinges, but his response had been crazy. What had she threatened that he couldn't stand to lose—his freedom? What the hell did that mean? If by freedom he meant the option to quit a job or a routine or an entire way of life whenever it palled, he had given that up long ago and gladly. Hopping from job to job was no more satisfying than he had realized hopping from woman to woman was. The teenaged Chris had thought of responsibilities and commitments as chains; the older Chris knew they were anchors to keep him from drifting through life, alone and rootless. Odin had given him a connection to the world, a tie that never chafed.

Lorelei would have done that for him as well, and he could finally admit the truth. With her enthusiasm and her unique insight on the world, she added spark to an existence that already had a lot of good in it. Moreover, she had reached beyond his public persona of foundation director, to the private Chris within him, and found there a big hole that even Odin hadn't filled. Yet he had thrown her out. No wonder she had finally turned cold. How much abuse could even the most giving woman take? He would never have treated the Duchess as badly, and she was just a heap of mechanical gadgets.

Chris came out of his dreary reverie and noticed that his heap of mechanical gadgets had developed a strange burr to its engine noise. He listened closely and checked all his instruments. Everything was normal. The noise had probably been his subconscious's way of warning him that he had been preoccupied with Lorelei too long for safety. A distracted pilot was a dangerous and endangered pilot. Chastened, he checked all the instruments again, then the skies around him. The puffy clouds had thickened to a gray sludge below. He hoped they would clear, as they were supposed to, before he had to start his descent. He radioed to a flight service station ahead for a weather report and was as-

sured that the skies over Teeterbrouck were clear and would
be when he got there.

He settled down and tried to keep his mind on flying. He
failed. The thought of losing Lorelei terrified him. Even
when the only contact they'd had was passing in the halls of
his house, he had gotten a lot of satisfaction from her presence. The prospect of her waiting for him had sped him back
from many a trip when he might otherwise have lingered
another day. But after the premiere she would have no reason to come back to Teeterbrouck. She would never again
search him out with questions and ideas. He'd never again
be able to set a fresh cup of coffee in front of her and see her
sweet smile light up, or watch her drive in each morning and
hop out of her dreadful car. He knew he had forged his own
fate, a fitting punishment for his stupidity. But deserving it
and bearing it were two different things.

The sudden asymmetrical drag of the airplane jerked him
back to reality once again. Something *was* wrong. Totally
alert now, he realized the Duchess was pulling sharply to the
left—he had lost an engine. He switched gas tanks—no response. He threw the crossfeed—still nothing. Okay, so it
wasn't a fuel problem...mechanical then, ice in the car-
buretor, perhaps. Whatever the cause, it took all his skill to
keep the little airplane trimmed and flying straight. One
engine couldn't keep him at this altitude and airspeed. Already he was dropping toward the muck of the weather below. How thick was the cloud cover? he wondered. Could
he fly under it? He pulled out a chart and found the radio
frequency of the nearest airfield. Now that he knew he'd be
in them shortly, the clouds looked ugly.

He felt no real fear for himself. He had always held the
philosophical view that when his time was up, it was up. But
he was bitterly sorry that, if he couldn't keep the airplane
aloft long enough, Lorelei would never know how much of
the past he would have liked to change.

* * *

Lorelei stood in the wings of the stage watching Rosie gallop through one of her well-known songs. The show was rolling: the VIPs had arrived by limousine amid an explosion of flashbulbs; the technical crews had signaled their readiness. The curtain had gone up on schedule and the premiere had begun—all without a word from Chris.

John Ward was closeted in a small office off of the command center calling every air-control tower between Manhattan and Rochester and asking for news of the Duchess. Lorelei had heard nothing from him since showing him how to use the phones. The running of the show had kept *her* running, but the worry festered in her mind.

When Rosie's song ended, the stage manager cued the set change and sent the first guest celebrity onstage. Lorelei glanced at her watch—7:55, right on schedule. The telecast of the documentary began at eight. If she hurried, she'd have just enough time to get to a television and see it start with her own eyes. She headed for the command post, mentally reviewing the sequence onstage: the ten-minute minidocumentary would be run, a second celebrity would speak, Owen Browne would introduce the film. One hundred and five minutes later, Rosie would bring out key people to thank—Chris had been scheduled as one of them—and then she'd close the show. Then invited guests and press would head for the splashy party Pioneer was sponsoring at the Waldorf.

Lorelei got to the command center a bit late. Sylvia stood watching a TV. "It's on, Lorelei. They started with coverage of the celebs coming into the theater tonight, then ran that interview they filmed with Rosie in the lobby, and the documentary's just started now. They're also going to have a panel discussion on world health issues afterward. Chris should be here to—'' She cut off the sentence sharply.